Carnival of Dead Girls

Flocksdale Files, Book Three

By Carissa Ann Lynch

Carnival of Dead Girls

Limitless Publishing, LLC
Kailua, HI 96734
www.limitlesspublishing.com

Formatting: Limitless Publishing

ISBN-13: 978-1-68058-461-5
ISBN-10: 1-68058-461-8

Dedication

To all of the "lost girls" out there…

Chapter One

Josie

I stood in front of an elongated mirror admiring the eighteen-gauge steel rings inside my newly stretched earlobes. The gaping holes were the size of a nickel, making the lobes look slightly distorted. The piercing artist advised against stretching them so quickly—it was supposed to be a *process*, she'd explained, in which you stretch the holes gradually over a period of time. But the hundred-dollar bill I placed on the counter was enough to change her mind.

I loved my new piercings, although they *were* sore, and couldn't wait to show my new friend, Freya. We'd been hanging out for a few months now, and the new piercings weren't my first attempt to impress her. Freya was hot, but not your typical beauty queen level of hot. She was dark and broody, her feelings fluctuating almost as often as her hair color—which this week was a combination of pink and orange, sort of like coral.

I knew she'd love the piercings, just like she loved my new wardrobe of all black and deep gray colors. Today I was wearing black again, and in conjunction with the piercings, I almost looked cool enough to hang out with a girl like Freya.

I thrust a knit cap down over my head, making sure it covered the entirety of my ears. It was nearly eighty degrees and sunny today. I'd just have to deal with the heat until I made it all the way to the bus stop.

My dad wasn't strict. In fact, he'd been pretty cool about accepting my recent wardrobe changes. It was my stepmom, Candy, I was hiding the piercings from. If she saw what I'd done to my ears, she'd freak out. Just like she did last summer when I came home with a teeny tiny stud in my nose.

They got married last year. *One* year ago. But that didn't stop the woman from trying to rule my life.

My real mother lived at Tokomo Penitentiary in Westwood, and she'd been locked up for six years now. Candy had taken it upon herself to assume the role of dutiful mother. I couldn't stand her, or how my father's behavior changed whenever she was around him.

I didn't need my real mom, and I didn't need a surrogate either.

I grabbed my messenger bag, swung it over my shoulder, and raced down the steps, making sure to secure the cap in place before passing my dad and Candy. They were sitting in the breakfast nook, sharing cups of coffee like a happy old couple. *Yuck.*

"Do you want me to drive you, Josie?" Candy asked in her sweet, pretending-to-be-my-mother voice. But I was already out the door, the screen door banging shut behind me. *Take that, bitch*, I thought angrily.

The bus stop was only one block from my house. The *house*—a classic saltbox design with rustic shutters and crimson-colored clapboards—was the largest house in the neighborhood. It was also the ugliest and most rundown. As though living in this *lame* town, ironically called Lamison Point, wasn't bad enough, I also had to live in that shit box.

Everyone in town knew about my mom being in prison, and their sometimes pitiful—sometimes disgusted—glances didn't go unnoticed by me. They looked down on me, felt sorry for me. And I hated them because of that. Maybe that's why I liked being friends with Freya so much. I loved her edgy style and "don't give a damn" attitude. She didn't care if my mom was in prison. She didn't give a damn about much of *anything*, really.

I cut through the Briars' front yard, trying not to stamp on any of their flowers or plants, because if I did, I'd hear about it later from my dad, or worse, from Candy.

I could see the kids lined up on Vermont Avenue, huddling in their cliques, gabbing away as they waited for bus 309. I jerked the wooly cap off, my twisted red locks tumbling down below my shoulders. I hated my hair. Naturally a brunette, I'd dyed it over the weekend. Like my ears, it was another attempt to impress Freya.

Approaching the bus stop, my eyes made a

beeline for her face. Freya stood amongst the other kids, but she emerged like a neon beacon of light. There were kids around her talking, trying to draw her attention, but she was too busy writing or drawing something in her notebook. She took notice of no one. Including me.

She was dressed in a black stretchy top and tattered black skirt, with holey knee-high socks and chunky black clogs. Her coral-colored hair was twisted in a loose braid that hung limply to one side of her pale, moon-shaped face, clearly unwashed and unbrushed. She didn't have to try to be cool or beautiful—she just was.

I stopped jogging, deciding instead to approach her with a cool stride. But then the bus screeched to a halt in front of the kids, and Freya jumped on before I had a chance to catch up with her.

That's okay, I thought. *I'll just talk to her on the bus.* But when I boarded, I was disappointed to discover she already had a seatmate in the back. I tried to catch her eye, to at least give her a wave or smile, but she was still busy, scribbling away in that notebook of hers.

Taking a seat up front, I smiled tightly at a kid with braces sitting next to me. I hadn't seen or spoken to Freya all weekend, and I thought she'd be eager to hang out. *But that's Freya for you. Hot and cold, and infuriatingly unpredictable.*

She was bubbly one minute, then quiet and withdrawn the next. And it frustrated me beyond belief. She hadn't even noticed my new piercings!

Although most days she seemed to genuinely like me, other days I wasn't so sure. We met at a party over the summer, and we'd been hanging out ever since…

I was sitting on a lopsided couch, nervously clasping a plastic cup filled with soda. Not usually one for parties, I felt anxious and awkward, alone. I'd decided on a whim to just go for it, get out of the house and meet people. Maybe I'd meet a guy or at least a friend to talk to. But showing up there, with all those people, just highlighted my weirdness, making me feel even worse about myself.

But then Freya showed up.

I saw her approaching—paving her own crooked path through a crowded living room of dancing bodies. Plopping down right next to me, she reached for my Coke and drained it.

"This ain't whiskey!" she cackled, jumping up from the couch. I expected her to leave, now that she'd discovered my lameness. But instead, she took my hands and began pulling. I thought she wanted me to dance, but she kept on tugging until we were out the door.

"Let's get out of here," she whispered, leading me away from my classmate's house. I couldn't even remember the name of the person throwing the party. We walked in silence, all the way to Mumston Park.

"This is my favorite tree," she finally said, breaking our silence. She was pointing at a massive, ancient tree, with limbs so twisted they almost looked fake. Like some crazy movie prop from Universal Studios.

Freya slipped off her shoes and began

climbing—as though she'd done it a hundred times. Reluctantly, I followed, my feet slipping on the bark as I struggled to catch up with her. When I reached her, she was up so high that the hot July air felt cool and damp. She was sitting on a branch smoking, attempting to make smoke rings by puckering her lips and pushing them out like a fish. I thought about the Cheshire cat in Alice in Wonderland, *and then she said, "Ever gone down the rabbit hole?" Like she was psychic or something. We sat in that tree till daylight. "You're my best friend," she mumbled as we parted ways for the night—night that had turned into day.*

I'd finally found a friend.

Or so I'd thought…I frowned, pushing away thoughts of that night. If I was honest with myself, I had to admit that every day and night since then had been a disappointment. At school, she was quiet and standoffish. Like today, she was so often in her own little world, far away from mine.

***

The rest of the school day went kind of like that—me trying to catch up with Freya, and Freya too busy and distracted to care. By the time I reached my last period of the day—study hall—I was pissed off and seriously depressed.

Study hall was the only class me and Freya had together, and I imagined that the next forty-five minutes would involve more of the same. *I'm not even going to talk to her. Or look at her. Maybe playing hard to get is the way to go with Freya anyway,* I sulked.

I found my usual seat in the back and opened a notebook of my own. Dug a charcoal pencil out of my bag, and started to draw with my head bent low down over the desk. I didn't see Freya come in the room, but somehow, I could sense her presence. Even from the back of the room. Rooms always got quiet when she arrived—boys admired her natural, careless beauty and girls either despised her for it or wanted to be her friend.

Instead of looking up, I kept on drawing, moving the pencil forward and back, in long, angry strokes. Drawing had been my main outlet for stress for as long as I could remember. I could still recall a day when I was six, and I opened the box of drawing pencils that my mother had clumsily attempted to wrap. Even before she went to prison, Brenda Crowley's presence in my life was spotty at best. Her job history was spotty as well, and I never knew when to expect a gift on my birthday, and when not to.

That particular year had been a good one for my mom—she didn't use many drugs that year and actually held a small job for a while, bagging groceries at the local Save-A-Lot. She and my dad were getting along that year, and I could remember that birthday when I received the pencils, and how it was one of the happiest days of my life. I imagined Mom and me leaning over the cake, blowing out my candles together. I'd wished for every day to be just like that one…

Those pencils were long gone now, worn down

to the nub like dozens of other sets that I'd previously owned. *Gone, but not forgotten, just like my mom...*

I scowled at the Freudian nature of my thoughts. Tried to focus solely on my drawing.

"Did you hear the news?" Freya asked. The sound of her voice, so close to me now, was startling. She was straddling the seat backwards in front of me, a big smile plastered across her face. She was always so moody that seeing her smile was like spotting a rare bird. I was so unused to seeing her grin that the image was sort of eerie.

"There's a carnival in town. It opens to the public tonight."

A carnival…I'd gone to an amusement park once with some friends, but I'd never been to a real carnival.

"What kind of carnival?" I asked.

"The *fun* kind, silly!" she said, tilting her head back and laughing so loudly that some of our classmates turned around to look at us.

"What's so funny?" I asked, still sore about her giving me the cold shoulder all day.

"Something fun happening in *Lames*ville, that's what." *Lamesville,* another one of our private jokes—about this town and the people who lived here.

"Wanna go?" she pressed, sticking out her lip with a pouty expression that not even a crazy person could resist.

"Sure." I shrugged. "Want me to come to your house at six?"

The bell rang, signaling the end of the school

day. Students began pushing their way out of the classroom.

"I'll meet you there," Freya shouted, taking off down the hallway. I tried to scurry after her, but eventually lost sight of her coral-colored hair in the thickening crowd.

Leaning against a row of lockers, I squeezed my eyes shut. That girl was so impossible! But despite being irritated by her aloofness, I couldn't help feeling a tiny glimmer of excitement about the carnival tonight.

"Nice house, dork," an upper classmen teased, pointing at the drawing in my notebook as he passed by. I stared down at the page.

Without realizing it, I'd drawn a picture of a creepy old house. I squinted at my own pencil strokes, trying to remember drawing it. It was a big house, sort of like mine, but different somehow. I slammed the notebook shut, my face reddening.

I headed for my own locker, but then stopped, noticing dozens of fliers sticking to the surface of random lockers throughout the hallway.

The flier read:

Carnival de Arcanorum. Come if you dare.

Shit! Freya didn't even say where to meet! I realized, feeling miserable.

But that wouldn't stop me from trying to find her. Who knows? Maybe the carnival would be fun…maybe it'd be a night I'd never forget.

Chapter Two

Freya was nowhere to be found when I boarded the bus. That was nothing new. She often rode home with older boys or classmates. The bus was filled with chatter, but my head felt empty. I rested my head against the side window, watching the hazy sun cast shadows on the hot black pavement as we whirred by.

My dad and Candy weren't home when the bus dropped me off. That was also nothing new. Candy managed a hip nail salon and my dad worked for some boring accounting firm. They both often worked long hours. I showered quickly, avoiding the blow dryer that sat on my sink. My thick red locks were impossible to manage and even harder to dry. I twisted it all in a big red knot, skipping makeup altogether, and stood in front of my crowded wardrobe closet, pondering. What to wear?

Rows of black tanks and t-shirts, along with black jeans, lined the closet. I shoved them aside. Stared at my favorite old Louisville Cardinals hoodie. *Oh, screw Freya and what she thinks of my wardrobe.*

My new piercings ached painfully as I set off on foot for the old elementary school parking lot. Sounds of the carnival drifted through the crisp fall air—sounds of clunking glass, chintzy amusement ride music, and children's laughter. I followed the noise and flashing lights, my Reeboks crunching up tiny pieces of recently fallen leaves. Halloween season was in the air.

The old parking lot was filled with game booths and tents, vendors peddling cotton candy, coins for rides, and glow-in-the-dark necklaces for kids. There was no way in hell I'd find Freya in this crazy crowd of Lamison's finest citizens—or the *lame-o's*, as Freya and I called them. There were hundreds of people strolling up and down the midway, checking out the game booths and buying food.

Beyond the booths was a huge canvas tent and a half dozen rides. Kids I recognized from school were lined up, waiting for their turn. Bumper cars, a carousel, a gray spinning disk, a fun house, and a couple small baby rides dotted the midway. A massive upright wheel as tall as the sky towered over all of them. I'd never ridden on a Ferris wheel, and I didn't want to try it today.

I could imagine Freya, sitting at the top of the Ferris wheel, scribbling in her notebook and ignoring the view. *Wouldn't that be typical.*

I saw more kids from school getting off a ride and called out to them, "Have you guys seen Freya?" But the blaring park music and sounds of the attractions made it impossible for anyone to hear me.

I headed back for the game booths, still looking around desperately. *Wow, I'm such a loser*, I thought. A young boy dressed in big floppy shoes and clown makeup was selling pink hard candy on a stick. I stopped him, grabbing the biggest piece from the bunch. The candy was hard on the outside with a gooey center on the inside. It tasted delicious. I walked, nibbling my candy, the bright, distracting lights making my head spin.

I watched a group of girls toss ping pong balls into tiny glass bowls of goldfish. *Poor fish*, I thought, smiling despite my mood. *I should be having fun too, not chasing some girl that doesn't even want to be my friend. What would Freya do if she were in my shoes?*

I already knew the answer to that question—Freya would play games or go in the funhouse; she would have fun with or without me. I decided to take a page from her playbook and do exactly that. *I'll just have fun on my own*, I thought markedly.

As though reading my mind, a short chubby kid with a goatee and glasses called out to me.

"Step right up! All ya have to do is knock over one of these milk bottles! And if you do, you'll win a stuffed animal!"

I shook my head no and kept walking, but the kid called out to me again.

"Your gauges are rad, girl!" The carny kid was the first person all day to even notice my new stretched piercings.

"Thank you," I said shyly, walking over to his booth. I pulled out some cash, deciding to play one game.

After several throws, the bottles were still standing. "Thanks," I said, nodding politely at the boy. I turned to leave, but then I had a thought.

"Hey, have you seen a girl with funky colored hair? She's real pretty, but dressed in all black with weird-colored hair and big chunky clogs? She's probably carrying around a big satchel and a notebook?"

"Oh yeah," the kid said. "It's hard to miss a hot chick like that, but that's not why I was watching her. Pockets was checking her out and following her around. And then he walked up to her, and I thought she would be all like 'Get away from me, loser,' but instead, she stood there talking to him, and they went into the Big Top together."

"Wait a minute," I said, holding up a finger in confusion. "Pockets is the name of a person? Is he one of the carnies...I mean, carnival workers?"

The kid laughed and said, "It's all right. We call ourselves carnies too. All you regular folks, we call you guys gillies."

I gave him another look that clearly meant for him to get to the point.

The kid explained, "Pockets is a guy who works in the Big Top." Seeing the confused look on my face, he further explained, "The Big Top is the big main tent, the one right behind me," he said, motioning with a jerk of his thumb to the enormous canvas-covered tent that lay behind the midway and was surrounded by a scattered cluster of smaller tents.

"Like I said, Pockets works in the Big Top.

Handles props and shit like that. He's a douche bag, and a young girl like that, well…she ain't got no business hanging out with a weirdo like him."

Hearing this, I felt a little worried about Freya. It wasn't unusual for her to make impulsive choices, and I didn't want some creep to hurt her. I took off jogging toward the Big Top.

"He's the one with the craters in his face, caused by acne scars and all that…" the boy called after me, but I was already darting inside the tent.

Chapter Three

The Big Top opened into a giant arena. I pushed my way through a thickening crowd, looking around for Freya. There were rows of seats surrounding the stadium. I climbed across the laps of countless patrons, finally collapsing in an uncomfortable royal blue seat.

I instantly felt ridiculous for coming inside. It was a stupid idea because the place was jam-packed and the chances of seeing Freya in these crowds were slim to none. If she was in some sort of trouble involving that creep "Pockets," there was little I could do for her here, crammed in the middle of an audience—an audience that had to be numbering in the hundreds by now.

The once sweet-smelling aroma of fried food and sweets was now replaced with the unmistakable fumes of ammonia, most likely released from animal waste. There were several horses, two elephants, and a camel in the center of the arena, and there were a handful of children in the middle of the ring, taking turns at riding on the animals' backs.

A man called out over a loudspeaker, announcing the show was about to begin. I scanned the wide space frantically, trying to find Freya—but no luck. All I could do now was sit back and watch the show, as there was no way I was climbing back through the stands to get out. I looked around for a man that might somehow fit the description of someone nicknamed 'Pockets,' but no one in particular stood out.

Sighing, I tried my best to get comfortable in the seat. *It's going to be a long night*, I thought, agitated.

The start of the show was marked by the grand entrance of several muscle-bound men in showy outfits, riding bareback into the arena. They did several mind-boggling tricks, like standing up on the horses, straddling two horses with only one foot on each animal's back, and flipping off mid-ride. I'd never seen anything like it, and for a moment, I just watched, spell-bound.

After the horse tricks, an elephant stood on a tiny pedestal and a tiger jumped through hoops. An extremely muscular man led a huge adult lion out to the center of the floor, then somehow coaxed the lion to do outrageous things, finally stunning the crowd into hushed silence as he used his hands to widen the lion's enormous mouth. And then he did the unthinkable, actually sticking his head into the wild animal's mouth. I closed my eyes, unable to watch. Covering my face with my hands, I ventured a peek through my fingers. Surprisingly, the lion didn't chomp down on the dumbass's head.

Next I watched nervously as a trapeze artist flipped through the air, barely catching the grip of her mate's hands. Several aerialists hung down from the rafters, and one of them was even suspended by her hair! Clowns on unicycles and astonishing magic tricks took up the next hour. When it was all over, I couldn't help wanting more.

My only wish was that Freya had been with me to enjoy the show.

The patrons slowly filed out of the arena, and I found myself once again scanning the crowds for my best friend. I was starting to think she might not want to be my friend anymore, certainly not my *best* friend. *You don't ditch someone who's supposed to be your best friend,* I thought, chuckling despite the hurtful truth behind the thought.

I followed the crowds out of the Big Top and noticed that most people seemed to be heading home, either on foot, or out to the exterior parking lot for those who came to the carnival in cars. I planned to do the same.

Freya had disappointed me again, and I was beginning to think I should just give up on her completely.

But just ahead, near the funhouse entrance, I caught a glimpse of pale orangish hair and tattered black clothing. "Freya!" I shouted impulsively. The Freya lookalike wasn't going in the funhouse. Instead she was headed for the ride that looked like a silver spaceship.

I shouted out again, but she didn't turn around. I watched her walk into the entrance of the strange-looking ride. *Fuck it,* I thought, deciding to follow her anyway.

Other kids were getting on, but as soon as I got to the ride's entrance, a whiskery old man placed his hand on my chest.

"Wait your turn. You'll go with the next group," he said gruffly.

"But—"

"No buts! Either wait, or go!" he half-shouted.

Ugh. What a douche bag! So, I had no other choice but to wait. I watched the disk go around and around, spinning for what seemed like a thousand turns. I could hear excited squeals and laughter pouring out. Finally, the disk got slower and slower, until it stopped.

Kids pushed their way through the exit. I waited for Freya to emerge, but she never came out.

That's strange. Maybe it really wasn't her I saw, I thought, just as the grumpy ride operator waved me inside.

I hesitated. There wasn't any reason to get on now. "Hurry, hurry, hurry!" the operator shouted, and two young girls behind me were pushing my back.

I'd expected there to be seats inside, but oddly, there were narrow sections for riders to stand against, and no seatbelts in sight. The sections were arranged in a circle, facing each other. And as soon as I found one to stand against, I spotted Freya on the other side. So, it *was* her I saw earlier. She'd apparently opted to stay on the ride and not get off. Her arms were draped around the neck of a much older man—a man with deep burn scars that looked almost like tiny little pockets in his skin. They were shamelessly kissing, groping each other in a way that grossed me out.

Yuck. He had to be nearly forty!

I considered walking over there, but then the floor swayed beneath me as the disk started spinning. I pressed my back against the cushion, bracing myself for the spin. I was expecting to feel off balance or clumsy. But that wasn't the case—I couldn't even move. The force of the spin held me pinned to the cushion, and it felt like a giant lying down on my chest, making my breath painful and slow.

I instantly hated the ride. The other riders' faces were a blur, but I immediately locked eyes with Freya. She saw me at the same time I looked at her, and her face broke into a smile. I tried to smile back, but my face felt droopy. I interpreted her smile as friendly, but then I realized she was laughing, saying something to her middle-aged date.

I watched her puffy lips moving, whispering in his ear. They moved slowly, and I tried to read what she was saying. "She acts like she's in love with me. Like I'm her girlfriend. Like a lesbian. Follows me like a lost little puppy…"

She giggled, but the man did not. He stared at me blankly, evilly. I tried to look away, my face reddening in shame from Freya's words, but my face was stuck to the seat. I was forced to stare in their direction, like some sort of sick, cruel joke. They watched me watching them, and laughed. I closed my eyes, waiting for the ride to stop. Waiting to get the hell away from Freya.

Chapter Four

The last person I wanted to deal with right now was my stepmom, Candy. But that's exactly who was waiting for me when I burst through the door at one o'clock in the morning. "Where have you been, Josie?" she demanded. "It's a school night!"

"I'm not your daughter!" I screamed, shoving past her and charging up the stairs to my second-floor bedroom.

I collapsed onto the bed, shoes and all, covering my face with a pillow. I was determined not to cry, but could instantly feel the gunk you get when you cry filling up my nose and throat.

I'd never felt so unhappy. I'd foolishly thought Freya was different from other girls, and that she wouldn't laugh at my awkwardness, that she actually wanted to be friends. But I'd been dead wrong, apparently.

I listened for the sound of my dad or Candy approaching the stairs to my room, but nobody came to check on me or scold me for my rude behavior. Truth is, I felt sort of bad for what I said to Candy, but it wasn't like I could take it back now.

When I closed my eyes, I could still see the gleaming lights of the carnival pulsating against the back of my eyelids, just like those treacherous strobe lights inside the spaceship ride. I tried not to picture Freya's puckered pink lips forming the words that hurt me so much. But the image of pouty lips pressed against the grotesque man named Pockets kept popping up again and again.

Pockets. *What a stupid name*, I thought, clenching my teeth in anger. I slid on a pair of lime green headphones, letting the beat of the newest Drake song take me away to another place, far away from the Carnival de Arcanorum—another stupid name. And far away from the thoughts of a girl who broke my heart and crushed my excitement of having a new friend.

***

I didn't see Freya the next day at school. She wasn't on the bus and I didn't spot her in the hallways.

But not seeing Freya was nothing new; she was known to cut class or just ditch school during the middle of a school day. I didn't try to look for her either. I walked with my head down, concentrating on my studies, and sketching with intensity whenever I had the chance. I wasn't big on confrontation, and didn't plan on "having it out" with Freya when I saw her. *If she'd rather kiss ugly freaks at that carnival than hang out with me, so be it.*

The Carnival de Arcanorum was all anybody at school could talk about, much to my dismay. Those who hadn't been to the carnival yet were planning to go tonight, and the ones who had were planning to go again. *Not me*, I thought gloomily. I never wanted to see that dreadful place again…

Instead of boarding the school bus at the end of the day, I decided to walk. The day was bright and sunny, leaves turning orange and red before littering the ground. The gorgeous weather was inconsistent with my black mood. I put my headphones on, secured my bag to my chest, and stared at my feet as I walked home. I mouthed angry lyrics to an Eminem song.

When I reached Vermont Avenue, I was so caught up in the lyrics of a different song about boulevards of broken dreams that I nearly ran right into a boy on a bicycle.

"Watch it!" the boy cried out, nearly tumbling off the bike as he swerved to avoid hitting me. When the boy looked up, I recognized him as the kid with the goatee from the game booth. He seemed to recognize me too.

"Hey," I said awkwardly. "I'm sorry. I wasn't watching where I was going."

"It's okay," the boy said. "I didn't mean to snap at you. I'm just not in a very good mood."

"Shouldn't you be at the carnival working?" I asked, wondering why the boy was so far away from the midway.

"I'm on break. My dad works at the carnival too, and he doesn't like me smoking. So, I'm just sneaking away to get a quick puff, if ya know what I mean. I'm Evan," he said, sticking out his hand.

I took his hand in mine. It was warm and chubby, but friendly. "I'm Josie," I said shyly.

"You coming back to the carnival tonight?" Evan asked, lighting up a cigarette and puffing deeply on its end.

"Nah…"

"Why not?"

Before I could answer, he said, "You really should come tonight. The freak show finally turned up a day late. All it costs is five bucks and you get to see cool stuff like fire-breathers and two-headed cats. Plus, my dad's letting me off around nine-thirty, so we could meet up and go through the freak show exhibits together. If ya want to, I mean…"

Honestly, I had no desire to return to the place of last night's trauma, but there was something about Evan…He seemed so desperate for a friend, kind of like me…

"Okay," I agreed, trying not to smile.

"How about we meet by the Ferris wheel around nine thirty?"

My smile grew. I was relieved to have someone who could actually make a set plan, for once.

"See ya then," he said, stubbing out his cigarette in a neighbor's half-barrel of butts.

"Yeah, I'll see ya," I said, surprised to realize that I was kind of looking forward to going to the Carnival de Arcanorum again.

Chapter Five

Evan was there at nine thirty sharp, waiting by the Ferris wheel, just like he said he would be.

"What's up?" I greeted him. I was dressed in a rosy pink cardigan with paper-thin white leggings. A far cry from Freya's choice of wardrobes for me.

"What do you want to do first? I was thinking we could wait until it gets real dark to go to the freak show. You wanna ride the Ferris wheel or the bumper cars?" Evan asked.

"Let's skip the Ferris wheel and go straight to the bumper cars," I suggested, not ready to face my fear of heights just yet.

"Okay," Evan agreed, and then we walked over to the ticket booth in the center area of the midway. We bought enough tickets to do the bumper cars and several other rides.

The bumper cars were a blast, and afterwards we tried our luck at some of the game booths. "All of these games are rigged," Evan said, laughing. "I shouldn't say that because you can actually win, it's just nearly impossible for most of these games."

Evan stopped at a concession stand, chatting with a young blonde girl he seemed to know behind the counter. When he turned around he had two free bags of cotton candy and two cans of soda.

"Thanks." I popped the top on the can and took a long swig of the drink. "So, tell me about working here. Do you like it?"

"Like isn't the word I'd use, but I've gotten used to this lifestyle. I never get to stay in a permanent location for long except for the couple of months we go home…We move from town to town like gypsies, and I've never had many friends because of it. My mom works in the Big Top, setting up dressing rooms and props, and my dad is a general laborer. He does a little of everything around here."

"I think it sounds kind of cool," I said, trying to make Evan feel a little bit better about his current predicament. "At least you get to meet different people and enjoy new landscapes." Evan chuckled.

"This is my only landscape," he said, opening his arms wide to indicate the carnival. "This is all I ever really get to see. My mom teaches me what I need to know for my schooling since I don't get to go like normal kids do, and I rarely do anything that doesn't involve the carnival in some way."

Deciding it was time to change the subject, I said, "Let's go to the freak show now."

Evan nodded and led the way.

The freak show was located in another large tent behind the Big Top. "All these other tents and campers are our living quarters…the people who work here, I mean…" Evan explained, motioning to the cluster of tents and trailers beyond the attraction tents.

"Which one is yours?" I looked at the tents curiously.

"Uh…you can't see it from here," Evan answered, and I realized he was embarrassed to show me his home.

"This is neat," I said, changing the subject again. I pointed at a creepy, gnarly sign with **'Freak Show de Arcanorum'** scrawled in blood-red letters.

There was a small marquee tent that opened into a spacious arena similar to the arena used for the Big Top show, but on a much smaller scale. A black-bearded gentleman with a top hat and tails was taking tickets in the front. He looked from Evan to me, and then nodded at us both, unhooking a thick velvet rope to pass through.

The arena was filled with an array of small booths and stages, set up as individual exhibits. "Let's start over there," I suggested, pointing to a booth at the farthest right end. I was already mesmerized by the scene laid out before me.

The first exhibit—the Human Pin Cushion—was a muscular bald man lying on a table, naked from the waist up. A "naughty nurse" look-alike inserted long prickly needles down the length of his arm. I scrunched up my face, cringing at the sight but unable to look elsewhere.

When she finished with that arm, she moved to the next. I couldn't take anymore. "Yuck," I said, grasping Evan's arm and pulling him toward the next display. I wasn't surprised to see the Bearded Woman sitting in the next booth. Children aged nine or ten were reaching out to stroke the wiry black hairs on her chin, but the woman seated behind the ropes didn't seem to mind.

"It's just a hormonal condition," Evan explained, smiling over at me.

"I feel so sorry for her," I said breathlessly, and I meant it.

"Don't feel sorry for her, Josie. Lucy—that's her name—is actually quite proud of her condition. And she has seriously profited from it. She even wrote a book about it called, *My Beard Is Sexy*." I turned to look at him, to see if he was being serious, and then we both burst out laughing.

The next several booths were more of the same. There were two little people, and a man so tall that he walked with his back hunched over, almost as though it was weighted down by bricks. There was a pair of creepy young boys who appeared to be a very real example of Siamese twins. "Do they live in these booths and cages?" I asked my new friend, suddenly feeling uneasy. Evan let out a low, hearty laugh.

"Hell, no! These freaks have their own living quarters and they choose to participate in these acts. They are the ones using their deformities and disabilities to exploit normal people and take their money, not the other way around."

I'd never thought of it that way, but had to admit that the kid had a point. However, I still couldn't help feeling saddened and sickened by each exhibit we passed.

In the middle part of the arena were contortionists and sword swallowers, working the crowded line of gawkers for tips. Evan and I stood watching, and I offered a small tip to a man breathing fire.

"You wanna get out of here?" I asked Evan.

"Yeah. But first, let me show you the last room over there." Evan pointed to a small wooden shack in the farthest left-hand corner. "There's nothing alive inside of it. Just really cool dead stuff, like the two-headed cat I told you about."

The way that he said it, so eager and maniacal-like, made me feel a little creeped out. But I had to admit that I kind of wanted to see the two-headed cat myself, so I followed him over to the grisly-looking shack.

The shack was attached to a much larger outbuilding that looked like a barn. I expected it to be huge when we went in, but only the little shack held display cases inside of it.

As Evan promised, the room was full of dead stuff. The biggest exhibit was a six-legged pony with glassy dead eyes in a large glass case in the center of the room. There were also several animals that seemed to have fish bodies attached to them instead of lower trunks and legs. It was obvious that some weirdo had simply sewn the heads onto fish tails. I don't know which seemed creepier—a half-animal/half-fish monster or some creepy psycho in a back room stitching it up.

I shuddered. I'd certainly had my fill of the freak show. Evan seemed cool, but this was a little too much. I looked over at my new friend, who seemed to be smiling as he strolled by the cases, running his hands over the glass as though he wanted to take one of the dead displays home with him.

There was a man sitting on a stool inside the shack, and I assumed he was the one in charge of this particular exhibit. When we came in I'd noticed a small wooden door in the back of the shack—probably leading into the barn I'd seen outside.

"What's back there?" I asked casually, making eye contact with the stern-looking man. He returned my stare blankly. "Not for you, kiddo. Move along," he said gruffly.

I looked over at Evan, expecting him to insist on going back there since he probably knew the guy, but Evan seemed ready to go now. He exchanged knowing glances with the man on the stool, then led me by my arm away from the shack.

Chapter Six

"Come on, let's ride the Ferris wheel!" Evan pulled my arm in the direction of the huge metal wheel in the sky. From here, it looked to be at least twenty stories high.

Despite my nerves, I allowed Evan to lead me straight to it, climbing into the first cart at the bottom. A metal bar closed over our waists, the metal clanking sound reminding me that it was too late to turn back now.

At least I won't die from falling since I'm locked in, I thought warily. *But I may have a heart attack.*

I sensed the sounds and movements of the ride whirring to life. Evan awkwardly sat beside me, his hands lying limply at his sides. I'd always imagined holding hands with someone when I rode the Ferris wheel.

The wheel started to turn, jerking the cart forward, and then we were lifted off the ground. I reached for Evan's hand desperately. My stomach filled with that feeling of butterflies. Not the good type of butterflies either.

We rose higher and higher, the cart swinging back and forth with the wind, the entire seat unsteady and creaky. Freezing in fear, I stared straight ahead, trying my best not to look down. *Get through this, and then you can relish in your bravery later*, I promised myself. *Just keep your eyes closed. Just keep your eyes closed*, I repeated over and over in my head.

But when we got to the tip of the very top, Evan shouted out, "Look, Josie! There's that girl you were looking for yesterday!" and those words left me with no choice but to open my eyes and look down.

The first thing I saw when I opened my eyes was a spectacular 360-degree view of Lamison Point. Never in my life had I been privy to a view like this. It was breathtaking. And terrifying…*Leave it to Freya to ruin this moment for me*, I thought sulkily.

My eyes drifted over to where Evan was pointing. Sure enough, there she was, standing a few feet from the freak show tent where we'd been only a few moments earlier. She looked tiny from up here, less intimidating…

Freya wasn't alone. She was arguing with someone, and even from here, I could see the bizarre contours of his face—it was that old guy, Pockets.

Freya leaned toward the man, wagging her finger angrily. I'd seen her like that before—she was pissed.

Suddenly, Pockets grabbed Freya by both shoulders, shaking her back and forth violently as he yelled.

"Hey!" I screamed, trying—stupidly—to stand up in the cart. "Freya!" I shouted, but no one could actually hear me from this elevation.

"Sit the fuck down! You're scaring me!" Evan hissed. The cart rocked back and forth dangerously. I quickly sat back in the seat, still trying to see what was happening with Freya and Pockets.

But the cart moved backward, descending back down from the top. As we passed the Ferris wheel operator at the bottom, I called out for him to stop the ride. I needed to get off and go help my friend!

But the operator didn't see me, and once again, the cart was jerking forward, heading to the top of the wheel. The wheel didn't stop at the top this time, but I caught a glimpse of the freak show tent area. Both Freya and Pockets were gone.

We circled back around nearly six times, but I never saw her again.

After exiting the Ferris wheel, I dragged Evan around the park, searching for Freya and/or Pockets. Evan was obviously irritated by this, but he tagged along, playing the role of dutiful friend.

Wherever Freya went, she's nowhere near here, I thought hopelessly. I wanted to make sure she was okay. *But why did I even care? Especially after what she said the other day*, a voice in the back of my mind scolded me. I thought about her lips moving, making fun of me for trying to be friends with her. *Lesbian*, she'd called me.

"Fuck it, she probably went on home," I said finally. I felt bad for ruining the Ferris wheel ride and dragging Evan around, so I agreed to ride a few more rides.

After getting jerked around on the bumper cars again, and then feeling like a human glue stick in the spaceship ride, I was ready to get the hell out of there. I said goodbye to Evan. Once again, the Carnival de Arcanorum had left a bad taste in my mouth.

Chapter Seven

By the end of the school week, I'd concluded that either Freya was totally ditching school or she was doing a damn good job of avoiding me. Since the Freya-sighting from the top of the Ferris wheel, I hadn't seen her, not even once. I wouldn't be surprised if she was cutting class to hang out with that old, gross boyfriend of hers, and in all honesty, I wasn't too worried about her.

Not until her mother showed up at my house asking questions.

When I got home from school on Friday evening, Freya's mother, Filomena, was sitting on the cotton fabric ottoman, next to Candy. "Hi," Filomena spoke softly, looking up at me with red-rimmed eyes. She was an older version of Freya, without the crazy-colored hair, purposefully tattered clothing, and goth-like makeup.

She didn't even wait for me to sit down before she started talking. "I haven't seen her in days, not since she left the house to meet you for the carnival. I know Freya can be a wild child, but she wouldn't run off without at least calling me. Her cell's been turned off, which is uncharacteristic for her. Please tell me you know something, Josie." Her eyes were pitiful, pleading.

I gave a sideways glance toward Candy. She was clutching Filomena's hand, her face scrunched up in worry. Normally, I'd want to call her out for being a phony bitch, but something on both of their faces told me they were being dead serious. They were scared.

So, I had no other choice...I told them everything I knew. Well, not *everything*. I told her that Freya was with a boy at the carnival, but I didn't tell her the boy was a *man*...and I also didn't tell her they were arguing.

I don't know why I held the details back. Perhaps, some part of me still believed Freya was just fine, and I didn't want to say anything to get her in trouble with her parents. *She'd really hate me then*, I thought glumly.

Filomena left, but only after making me promise to call her if I heard from Freya. I sat in my room, chewing the inside of my own cheek until it was raw and bleeding. I had to take matters into my own hands. I had to go back to the carnival.

I left through the front door without saying goodbye to my dad or Candy. I didn't walk to the carnival—I ran.

If something had happened to Freya, it would be all my fault for not sticking around and making sure she was okay the other night. *Yeah, she said some shitty things...but I still wouldn't want any harm to come to her.*

I had to find Pockets and Freya, settle this confusion once and for all.

The houses I passed flew by in a blur as I ran with a quickness fueled by intense anger. It was anger toward Freya for screwing me over…and anger toward Pockets for taking advantage of her, and for putting his hands on her the other day. Anger toward myself for giving a damn about Freya…

I stopped short as I reached the edge of the abandoned school zone. The lot was empty.

All of those rides and games and booths…all of those people…

How the hell did they get out of town so quick? If not for the scraps of candy, traces of streamers, and popped balloon particles, I never would have believed that such an enormous carnival had been right here, in this very spot, just a couple days ago.

My heart was racing, pounding so hard in my chest that it ached.

The carnival was gone. Pockets was gone. And Freya was gone along with him.

Chapter Eight

Coming up with the plan was the easy part. Putting it into action was where things got tough. Screeching to a halt, I parked my bike in front of the local library. *Please be open*, I wished, crossing my fingers as I reached the entrance door. It was a dull one-story building, the same **'Nelson County Public Library'** sign hanging on the door, along with a list of warnings. Don't enter without shoes. No cell phones or food, etcetera. I muttered a silent prayer of thanks as the door swung open wide before me.

It was so early the sun wasn't out yet, but old Miss Hamm was manning the front desk. I smiled at her politely. She'd been working the library counter for as long as I could remember. Flashes of her younger self sporting a beehive came to mind. All I knew was that she'd been the only librarian since I was a kid.

Miss Hamm was an intimidating woman, and the kids at school were slightly frightened of her. I was no exception.

"Is there a computer terminal open?" I asked, resting my hands on the front counter, mindful to keep my elbows back. Silently, she pointed to a row of large computers near the magazines. They were seriously out-of-date.

"Thanks, Miss Pig…Miss Hamm, I mean…" I said, nearly calling her by her local nickname, "Miss Piggy," for her large yellow curls and snout-like nose.

My big master plan was to use the internet to search for The Carnival de Arcanorum. Very original, right?

Surely I'd be able to find some sort of show schedule with dates and locations for the carnival's next event. If I knew which town they were scheduled to appear in next, then I could track down Pockets and question him about Freya.

I typed the words "Carnival de Arcanorum" into the Google search box. Instantly, I was taken aback when I found no listings for a carnival by that name.

There were multiple listings for other carnivals and online carnival games, and even a Latin word translation website, but no website for the Carnival de Arcanorum, and no hits mentioning its name.

Flabbergasted by the lack of results, I clicked on the Latin translation website. I was surprised to learn that the word "arcanorum" meant "secret" in English.

As though that really helps me. They're so secretive that they can't be found! I thought, exasperated.

Despite the setback, I was still determined to search out the Carnival de Arcanorum. There had to be another way.

Next, I typed in "Freak Show de Arcanorum," but again, no luck. I even went so far as to type in the name "Pockets" and "Evan" paired with the term "Carnival de Arcanorum," but once again wound up disappointed.

I searched every social media site I could think of for the carnival or names of its workers I could remember. Shockingly, there was still nothing.

Who didn't have a social media profile these days? I wondered, irked by the fact that I was getting nowhere with this search. Despite my disappointment, my determination remained intact—nothing would stop me from finding Freya. I just needed to figure out another way to track down the carnival.

***

It was not until three o'clock in the morning that I remembered the name of the bearded woman. Her name was Lucy. I jerked out of bed, yanking on a pair of scruffy sweats. It was the middle of the night—a *school* night—but that didn't stop me from climbing down the tree limb outside my bedroom window and hopping onto my bike in the rain…

When old Miss Hamm arrived at work that morning, she was less than pleased to find a sleeping girl on the concrete steps to the library. She nudged me with a brown loafer. Startled, I quickly got to my feet, rubbing the sleep from my eyes. I looked around, confused initially. But then I remembered I was at the public library. *Lucy.*

Miss Hamm said nothing, but she unlocked the door and held it open for me. I tried to be patient as she brewed a pot of coffee. Although I never drank the stuff, I accepted the warm mug she offered me.

With the first sip, my face crumpled. Thankfully, Miss Hamm was there, offering me a cube of sugar.

"Okay," she said, taking a seat at the small work station beside me. "Tell me what this is about, young lady."

My initial plan was to just tell her about the book and ask for her assistance in finding it. But before I knew it, I was spilling out the entire story to old Miss Hamm.

"Have you reported all of this to the police, Josie?" she asked, her brows furrowing slightly.

"Yes." And it was the truth. Yesterday—after Freya had officially been announced as missing— her mother, Filomena, had filed a police report. Detective Sanchez had interviewed most of Freya's classmates already, including me. Despite my earlier reservations about not wanting to get Freya in trouble, I'd told Detective Sanchez what I knew. If holding back information impeded the investigation, I didn't want to be responsible for it. All I wanted to do was find Freya, and that meant being honest with the adults that could help with the search.

"Well, it sounds like the police are investigating already, Josie. You should trust them to do their jobs." Miss Hamm looked at me sternly.

"I just need to find this book and more information about the author that wrote it. If I find out anything useful, ma'am, I will certainly contact

Detective Sanchez immediately."

She pursed her lips, but then finally seemed satisfied that I was telling the truth.

The library was completely deserted at this early hour. For that, I was grateful. "Now tell me the name of this book," Miss Hamm stated matter-of-factly, her long, wiry fingers poised in a perfect typing pose over the keyboard.

I sighed, closed my eyes, and braced for the embarrassment. "*My Beard Is Sexy*, that's what it's called."

I opened my eyes and glanced over to gauge her reaction, but surprisingly—and thankfully—she took it in stride, and was hard at work typing.

"And what did you say the author's name was again?" she asked.

"Lucy something. I don't know her last name. Does that mean we won't be able to find the book?" Like a popped balloon, I could feel all hope dissipating.

"Oh, I'll find it. Don't worry," she said, clicking away at an angle I couldn't see. I was tempted to walk around the library desk and take a peek, but I imagined her smacking my hand with a ruler or something if I did so.

Minutes passed and then finally, she swiveled around in her chair.

"Lucinda Livingston. That's her name. She is the author of *My Beard Is Sexy* and another children's book of assorted fairytales. What do you want to know about her?" she asked, obviously proud of herself for solving my mystery.

"Everything!" I squealed. Maybe I could track

down Freya after all! But first I had to track down the Carnival de Arcanorum.

Miss Hamm started to tell me all about the author. Her age, where she was born, her astrological sign…

"Wait," I said impatiently. "For now, can you just tell me where she lives?"

"A town called Flocksdale. It's a sparsely populated area. About two hundred miles from here…Wait. You don't think this lady kidnapped Freya, do you?" she asked worriedly.

"No, I don't," I assured her. "But she might be the only real connection to the carnival."

I gathered up my messenger bag and handed the empty coffee mug back to Miss Hamm. "Thanks for your help," I said.

"Now, make sure you relay this information to Detective Sanchez if you think that it's important, okay? Don't try to pursue any leads on your own," she told me, staring me down in a way that reminded me of a hawk observing its prey.

"I won't," I lied, heading for the door.

Chapter Nine

I chewed slowly, trying to enjoy my favorite dinner—roast, potatoes, and green beans—with Dad and Candy. But the food was tasteless. I was distracted, focused on getting this meal over with as quickly as possible. Plans had been made.

Candy seemed quieter than usual. She'd been that way ever since my outburst the other night. If I were my stepmom, I wouldn't like me much either.

Even though I felt guilty, tonight there was no room for distractions.

After dinner, I helped Dad with the dishes, took a shower, and rushed through my calculus homework. Finally, it was time for bed. I kissed Dad on the cheek and offered Candy an awkward half-hug.

I lay quietly on my bed for nearly two hours, making sure they were sound asleep. I tip-toed over to my closed bedroom door, pressing my ear to its paint-chipped surface. Met with dead silence, I breathed a sigh of relief.

I grabbed a handful of shirts, shorts, socks, and

underwear from my bureau drawers, then folded them carelessly and slid them inside an oversized duffel bag. I packed a couple more things—my toothbrush and some toiletries. Most importantly, I grabbed my roll of cash that I kept in a shoebox beneath my TV stand. I'd been saving money for a while now, earned from my weekly allowance and odd jobs for my neighbor Beatrice. It wasn't a lot of money, but it was enough to get me where I needed to go.

Sleeping for a while would be the smart thing to do, but I was too revved up to even think about closing my eyes. I sat in the dark, watching the hands on the clock sluggishly tick by, waiting for five o'clock to roll around. Dad and Candy usually slept until at least seven, so I didn't worry much about them waking and catching me.

Alas, it was time. I grabbed my duffel bag and climbed down the tree limb for a second night in a row. I was less worried about waking my parents, and more concerned a nosy neighbor—like Beatrice, for instance—would catch me in the dark. So I moved swiftly, mounting my bike and pedaling away from my street and Vermont Avenue as quickly as possible.

It took me nearly an hour to make it to the bus stop, and I nervously approached the ticket box, worried that I might be too late to catch the six o'clock bus. The lady took my money, frowning all the while. I'll never understand why so many unpleasant people work in customer-driven fields.

The ticket turned out to be pricier than I'd expected.

"Which one is it?" I asked, adjusting my bag tiredly and staring at the rows of buses.

"That one'll take you to Flocksdale," the ticket taker said, pointing without looking, a scowl on her face.

I yawned. *Flocksdale, here I come!*

Chapter Ten

With a five-hour ride ahead of me, I had plenty of time to get caught up on sleep. And I definitely needed some, considering the fact that I'd barely slept in two days. The smells and sounds of the bus made it nearly impossible, though.

I pulled out my sketch pad, hoping that the familiar act of drawing would ease my mind. My thoughts were spinning, filled with concern for Freya and guilt for taking off without telling Dad.

Without realizing it, I'd begun to sketch the image of Freya's face. Despite her beauty, she always seemed to wear a sad, troubled expression. *Maybe deep down, she always thought something bad would happen to her and that's why she was so melancholy all the time…*

But that seemed ridiculous. *And who said anything bad has happened to her, anyway?* I scolded myself.

I usually liked to draw with charcoal pencils, but today I took out a handful of colored ones so I could sketch in the color of her hair. The color had changed so much lately—green one day, red the next, and then coral-colored last time I saw her.

I self-consciously ran my fingers through my own mess of bright red locks. *Who was I fooling? Did I really thinking changing my hair color, getting piercings, and donning all black would make Freya like me?*

Sketching with intensity now, I made her hair wild and ugly. Then I added deep lines and craters in her face to match Pockets'. Ugh. *You stupid bitch! Why am I chasing you across the country when you don't even deserve it?* I wanted to shout at the putrid drawing of Freya's face.

Finally, I scribbled out her eyes and nose, as well as those red, pouty lips. I drew an X over the drawing, then slammed the notebook shut.

I closed my eyes, finally giving in to my exhaustion.

***

I woke up just in time to hear the bus driver announcing my stop over the intercom. Stretching my legs, I made my way to the front of the bus, banging people's kneecaps with my own.

I stepped off the bus, thrilled to escape the reeking smell of sweat and too much perfume. The bus instantly pulled away, leaving me stranded in the middle of a heavily wooded area. The road I'd arrived at was wide, but empty. I looked back and forth for street signs or buildings—nothing. *Why in the hell did the bus driver dump me off here?* I wondered angrily.

I headed west, in the direction the bus went, adjusting the chafing duffel bag on my shoulder. *At least the weather's nice*, I thought, walking at a steady pace.

The road was surrounded by an immense canopy of trees, creating a strange "tunnel" of sorts around me. The woodsy surroundings reminded me of a camping trip I took a couple years ago with Dad. It was the last real outing we had together before he married Candy. I felt a sharp pang of guilt thinking about my dad. He and Candy would be worried sick by now, discovering my bed empty when they got up. The last thing I wanted to do was cause them pain. But the sooner I found Freya, the sooner I'd be able to get back home to them.

I followed the tree-lined road for nearly a mile before finally spotting signs of civilization. A hand-painted welcome sign greeted me in the distance, and at first I couldn't read the words, but as I got closer I could. **'*Flocksdale.*'** It sounded vaguely familiar, although I couldn't recall anything noteworthy or memorable about the town.

Well, why didn't the driver bring me here? I thought, stopping to stare at the weathered sign. Strangely, I nodded at it as though it were a person, just happy to be in a town, as opposed to walking in the woods.

My plan was to borrow a phone book and look up the address for Lucinda Livingston. The main street was lined with old-fashioned buildings, housing small restaurants and shops, as well as a used bookstore.

Thrilled to see a small Marathon with one single

pumping station, I headed inside to ask for a phone book. But the lady at the counter offered me something even better. Considering the fact that the town only had a population of two hundred, she knew who Lucy was as soon as I mentioned her name.

Moments later, with a can of soda and a bag of chips in tow, I headed down the main street, looking for Saints Road. It was a mile-long walk from the convenience store, according to the helpful woman who worked there. I'd just finished walking a mile and now another lay ahead of me. However, I didn't mind it much. The town was quaint, with rows of shotgun and ranch-style houses.

All of the kids were still in school apparently, but I noticed several nice-looking adults walking dogs and riding bikes along Flocksdale's crumbly sidewalks.

The girl told me to walk toward the river, but as soon as I saw it, to hang a left and then a right on Saints. It wouldn't be too hard to find.

Less than half an hour later, I was standing in front of a rundown, two-story house with an attached garage and well-kept yard. I'd been so focused on finding Lucy's home that I had no idea what to do or say once I got here. I mean, the carnival obviously wasn't in town. Lucy traveled with the freak show and wouldn't be here.

What did I hope to find? Certainly not Lucy or Freya.

Maybe Lucy has family here or one of her neighbors can tell me how to reach her, I thought hopefully. I stared at the rundown house—it was just like the girl in the store had described.

I trudged up the concrete driveway, deciding just to wing it. Who knew? Maybe nobody would even answer. I rang the bell, setting down my bag to relieve my raw shoulder.

Several awkward minutes passed before a cute blonde girl threw open the door, staring at me blankly. "Who the hell are you?" she demanded.

"I…uh…" I was caught off guard by her brashness. Clearing my throat, I said, "I'm looking for Lucy Livingston. Do you know where to find her? I'm Josie."

The girl eyeballed me strangely before asking, "Who wants to know?"

Here's the thing—I'm a terrible liar. There was no use beating around the bush. Just like I did with Miss Hamm, I blurted out the whole story. About Freya and Pockets, and my fears that she'd been kidnapped by him or one of the other carnies.

"Look, I just thought that if I found Lucy, then maybe I could find the carnival and Freya. I'm really sorry for bothering you…" I turned to walk away, feeling stupid, and my face a dark shade of red.

"Lucy's my mom," the girl called out from behind me. "But she's not here right now. They're coming back for Halloween in two days. She always comes home for my fall break from school, and they put on the carnival show for our townsfolk for a week. The whole crew stays here for a few months and then they hit the road again," she said, rolling her eyes. "'Touring'—that's what she calls it, with that stupid fucking freak show of hers. And while she's gone, I'm stuck here living with my stepdad," she spat angrily.

"I don't like my stepmom, either," I said softly. We both stood there silently, sizing each other up. Sharing some sense of camaraderie.

"My mom calls every night from the road. I'll tell her you came looking for her," she said. I stood there, chewing my lip. I didn't want to spook Pockets or Freya. Maybe it'd be best if I just waited for a few days until the carnival came home for Halloween.

"No, please don't tell her. I think I'll just wait till they get to town. Try to find my answers then. Thank you though," I said, heading back out to Saints Road. I had no idea what I'd do for two days until Halloween arrived.

Suddenly, I heard the sounds of leaves shifting behind me. The blonde girl was running after me. "Hey, wait up! I'll walk with you," she offered cheerily.

The girl seemed nice and all, but I had work to do. Not to mention the last time I made a friend she accused me of being a lesbian…I smiled tightly at her, willing myself to be friendly.

Chapter Eleven

I set out on foot, heading back the way I came. The strange girl fell in step beside me. I focused on the road ahead, feeling a strange mixture of fear and exhilaration. If the carnival was coming home in a couple days, then I could confront Pockets and hopefully, find out where Freya went.

"Aren't you going to ask my name? I mean, you told me yours and all…" the girl asked bluntly, struggling to keep up with me. She was nearly a head shorter than me with glittery, childish sneakers. I stopped abruptly, facing the girl.

"Okay, I'll bite. What's your name?" I asked tiredly.

"Rachel." She shrugged as though my question was dumb and she wasn't the one who prompted me to ask it in the first place. I rolled my eyes and kept walking.

When we reached the end of Saints Road, I took an immediate left, following a street called Lincoln Boulevard, according to its sign.

After a few yards Rachel stopped. "Okay. Where

are you going?"

I kept on, ignoring her.

"You're not from around here. You don't know anybody here. You *appear* to be alone. So, where in the hell do you plan to stay for the next couple nights until your girlfriend shows up?"

I jerked around. "She's *not* my girlfriend! I'm not a lesbian!" I shouted defensively.

Rachel held her hands up. "Whoa. I never implied that you were a lesbian. And even if you were, who cares? I'm not a bigot. I meant she's a girl and she's your friend. Am I wrong about that? She is your friend, right?"

I'd been working up a sweat ever since I got off that bus. Using both hands, I swiped the grime away, breathing deeply. I hadn't meant to snap at her. I guess I was just a little defensive about what happened with Freya the other day.

Rachel was still trying to apologize, even though she did nothing wrong. "I mean…you must really care about her, or else you wouldn't be taking a bus cross country to find her," she said.

"Listen, I'm sorry. I didn't mean to jump down your throat. Actually, Freya's a pretty rotten friend. I don't know why I'm trying so hard to find her…I guess I just wish I had a friend who cared enough about me to do the same, if I disappeared like that…"

"Well, come on then," Rachel said, tucking her arm in mind. "I know somewhere you can stay, but you probably won't like it…"

***

It didn't take long for me to notice the houses that lined the streets of Flocksdale. There was a strange bit of inconsistency in the way they looked, unlike the normal houses near the center of town.

Some of the houses looked newer, freshly built. They were designed in a modern style. But others were sitting up high on stilts, as though they were built to survive a major flood. I'd noticed a river as we crossed Baumans Lane.

Stranger still, there were dozens of houses surrounded by scorched earth with deep black scars.

"What the hell happened here?" I asked. Rachel smirked.

"A few years ago, a bunch of crazies escaped from the asylum and burned half the town to the ground. Before the fires, many of the houses were torn down…and before that there were floods. This town's been through hell. You can't destroy us, drown us out, or burn us down. This whole town is like one giant cockroach."

"Wow," was all I could say, as we strolled down a road called Clemmons Street. I could see an enormous Victorian home sitting at the street's end, severely damaged by fire. The block surrounding it was devoid of houses, as though no other homes survived and the owners didn't bother to rebuild.

"I take it nobody wanted to rebuild by this house," I said, chuckling nervously.

"You don't know how right you are," Rachel mumbled.

I slowed down, thinking we'd taken a wrong turn. But Rachel kept moving forward, headed for the creepy, condemned house. "Where are we going? I thought you said you knew somewhere to stay?"

She halted, raising her eyebrows at me. She looked from me to the house, and back again.

"You have to be fucking joking," I said, stopping dead in my tracks.

"Look, nobody lives there. It's completely abandoned. Plus, this is where the carnival will be. They set up shop here—on this street—since there's no other houses around. The House of Ho—*This* house, is what they use as their haunted house attraction."

I still didn't budge. No freaking way was I staying in that freaky dump of a house by myself, in a town where I knew no one.

"Look, I'd let you stay at my house, but my stepdad doesn't know you, and he knows everyone in this town. You said you wanted to stay inconspicuous, so that the carnival workers wouldn't know you were here. Well, this is the only place I know to stay. It's not like we have hotels or fancy bed and breakfasts around here. We're lucky we still have a McDonald's."

"I'll stay with you," she added, surprising me.

"You'd do that for me?" I asked, crossing my arms over my chest.

"Well, I'd want someone to do the same for me if I were in your shoes." She winked.

I stared at the dilapidated mansion, my heart racing. I swallowed a painful lump in my throat, looking at my new friend.

"Okay. I'll do it," I said, surprising myself.

Chapter Twelve

It was only an hour till nightfall, but my stomach was growling noisily. "Look, can you stay here for like thirty minutes by yourself? I'll go get snacks, drinks, some flashlights, and candles," Rachel offered hesitantly.

The last thing I wanted to do was hang out at this scary, abandoned house by myself. But what choice did I have? It's not like we could stay here all night without lights or food. The thought of being in that house in the dark was worse than hanging out for an hour in the daylight.

"Okay." We were standing next to the house now. I stared at the angry black swipes and crumbled bricks. The fire had done a lot of damage, but its external structure seemed sound. "Are you sure it's safe here? I mean, the ceiling w-won't collapse, will it?" I stammered.

"Nah. It's a dump. Burned up inside too. But this beast of a house won't fall down. I don't think an F5 tornado could take it down," she said, gazing at the house alongside me.

I walked around to the backside, observing a skinny alleyway and a beat-up, old floodwall behind the house. Scribbly words—graffiti—covered half of the wall. I squinted at the words, trying to read them. They didn't look like the English language.

"*Qui autem intrat non egrediar*," I struggled to pronounce the words.

"It means 'He who enters won't come out,' " Rachel said softly from behind me.

"How do you know that?" I stared at the angry letters, barely breathing. Someone had written them here, long ago.

"Because in a town this small, there's not much else to do. It's Latin. I bought a book from the bookstore and translated it. Easy as that."

I thought about the carnival name on the flier when they came to Lamison Point. *Carnival de Arcanorum*, another Latin word.

"What does it mean? I mean, why would somebody write that here?" I asked, a gust of wind causing me to shiver.

She simply shrugged.

Beyond the wall, a river gushed. I spotted a decrepit walking bridge in the distance.

"What the hell happened over there?" I pointed at what appeared to be a burned down factory across the river. "How did fire reach *both* sides of the river?"

"Like I said, it was a bunch of crazy girls that did it. They burned that one down first, then came across the river..." she said softly, her voice far away and thoughtful.

"This place is the pits," I added, frowning.

"That's putting it lightly…Okay, well I'd better hurry if I'm going to get the flashlights and stuff," she reminded me. I nodded, dreading her departure.

"Is it okay if I just sit out here while you're gone?" I asked, pointing at the river. I wasn't ready to venture inside the house without her next to me.

"Sure. I don't think anyone will see you, anyway. Nobody comes down this street, except when the carnival comes to town."

I took a seat on the edge of the riverbank, watching Rachel's form grow smaller and smaller in the distance. I couldn't imagine sleeping two nights in this place, and I didn't really want to think about it. *And all because of stupid Freya*, I thought, slumping miserably as my teeth chattered from the cold.

Chapter Thirteen

"It'll be fun. Kind of like a sleepover!" Rachel gushed excitedly. She carried a heavy-looking backpack, as well as two blankets in her arms.

We were still outside, watching the sun go down. The deserted street was deathly quiet. Eerie.

"Not to mention the fact that when I tell everyone at Plainview—that's where I go to school—they're going to think I'm such a badass," she went on.

The October air was cool, icily crisp. Instead of slowing down, the river water whipped and whirled, angry waves slashing against the muddy river banks. Outside or inside—this place was creepy.

"Okay, I'm ready," I said, relieving her of the blankets. "How do we get inside?"

"This way," Rachel said with a wink, leading the way to the other side of the house. The earth around the house was scorched black, no plants or flowers to be seen.

"This window's open," she said, pointing at a narrow, old-fashioned sill.

"So you've been here before?" I asked, confused.

"Look, I've never stayed here by myself, but I've snooped around a bit during the daytime. One day, like six months ago, I found the front door unlocked. That's when I ran in and unlocked this window. I knew someday I'd have the guts to actually come inside…"

I raised my eyebrows, not impressed with her bravery. I'd thought she was being good-natured by volunteering to come with me. But as it turns out, I was the excuse she needed to fulfill some sort of weird fantasy about sleeping in haunted houses.

She lifted up on the window, eager to get inside. It didn't budge.

"Welp, looks like your dream come true isn't happening tonight." I whirled around, heading back out to the street.

Fuck this. Ready to go home, I thought about my nice, comfy bed and my dad's shish kebabs. Freya wasn't worth it…

But then I heard a crunching sound, like paint breaking, and when I looked back, the window was open.

"Just needed a little elbow grease!" Rachel grinned as she propped herself up and over the sill.

I hesitated. I didn't want to leave her in there alone…

Groaning, I walked over to the window, tossed the blankets through the hole, and climbed inside the strange house, praying I didn't live to regret this.

Chapter Fourteen

I was in what I guessed to be a sitting room, although there was no furniture to be seen. Rachel stood there gripping a Maglite, grinning as though she'd known all along that I'd follow. I narrowed my eyes at her.

"No furniture?" I asked, gathering up the blankets. The floor was hardwood, angry black scorch marks smearing their once glossy surface. My voice bounced off the walls, echoing throughout the empty space.

"I'm not sure. But when I've looked through the windows, I've never seen much. I think most of it burned up."

"I thought you said you came in and unlocked the window?"

"Yeah, well…I ran like hell, in and out. Nearly scared myself to death," Rachel chortled.

I couldn't help smiling. "Give me one of those," I said, pointing at her flashlight. She set her backpack down, digging around for another one. She handed me a smaller version of hers, as well as a bottle of water.

"Any food in there?" I asked. She dumped its contents out, revealing a couple candy bars and squished packs of crackers. I was so hungry I didn't care.

I opened the crackers up, pouring the crumbs in my mouth.

We plopped down on the floor, finishing off the food and sipping our water.

"So, what did you tell your stepdad?" I asked curiously.

"Ah. I told him that I was going to my friend Taylor's house. I stay there a lot on the weekends, so it's not a big deal." She stared at me, assessing me for something.

"And what about you? Where do your parents think you are, Josie?"

I took another drink of water. "They don't know where I am. I just took off, rather impulsively I'll admit, but I thought maybe Freya was kidnapped and I felt like it was my fault…"

"Why would it be *your* fault?" she asked. I sighed. The last thing I wanted to do was tell my new friend about what happened between Freya and me at the carnival.

"We had a disagreement is all. And then I was sitting at the top of the Ferris wheel and I saw this guy—Pockets—man-handling her. They were arguing. I couldn't find her afterwards, but I was so mad that I just left, not thinking twice about it… But then she didn't come to school all week and now the police are looking for her. So, maybe I wanted to be the hero…My way of making it up to her and myself for just leaving like that."

"I know who Pockets is," she said nonchalantly.

"You do? Is he a bad guy?"

"Yeah, he's an asshole. But I still can't see him or any of the carnival workers kidnapping a girl."

I chewed at my nails thoughtfully. Maybe this was a stupid idea. Maybe Freya rebelled, ran away on her own. Maybe this was an attempt to get attention. Well, if so, she'd succeeded.

"I can't believe I'm going to sleep two nights in this place," I said, looking around the black room. The flashlights sat between us, making our faces exaggerated, ghost-like.

I picked my light up, shined it around the room. It was empty besides remnants of wallpaper and blackened floor boards. "Let's look around," I suggested.

Rachel's eyes widened. I expected her to say no, but she nodded okay. We walked through the rooms on the first floor, our flashlights held out in front of us. Now that the sun was gone, it was getting more and more chilly. I wished for one of those blankets back in the sitting room.

I don't know if I imagined it or not, but there seemed to be a strange smell in the air. I sniffed loudly.

"Smells like something burning, right?" Rachel asked.

I nodded. It seemed crazy that it could still smell so bad years later.

The rooms were mostly empty, remnants of bedroom furniture in one room and a cast iron bath tub standing strong in one of the bathrooms.

"Who lived here?" I asked, staring at the eerie fragments of a kitchen counter.

"Ah. Lots of people," she said vaguely.

"How many?" I asked, approaching a grand set of blackened stairs. I took a few tentative steps, Rachel pushed me forward.

"Well, it used to be owned by the Garretts. A sick, twisted group of fucks. They tortured girls and stuff. That's why they call it the House of Horrors."

I immediately dropped my flashlight. It clattered loudly on the stairs and went rolling, off toward one of the bottom-floor rooms.

"Why the fuck didn't you tell me that?" I asked angrily. "Get me the hell out of this place!" I screamed, scurrying past her down the stairs.

I reached the bottom of the stairs, and immediately began groping for my flashlight on the floor. Finally, I got down on my knees, crawling around to find it.

That's when something hit me over the head.

Chapter Fifteen

"Oh my god! Are you okay?" Rachel screamed in the dark.

I moved around, trying to unpin myself from whatever had fallen on top of me.

Rachel stood over me now, shining her flashlight in my face. "Holy shit. The whole light fixture came down on you. Don't move. I'll get it off," she assured me.

The dome-shaped light wasn't heavy. When it struck me, it was just so shocking. I pushed it off easily, without any help.

"I'm so sorry, Josie. I'm sorry I brought you here and put you in danger," Rachel moaned.

"It's not your fault." I stood up shakily, rubbing the sore spot on my head.

"Let me see," she demanded, turning me around and shining the light on my head. "Looks like a goose's egg, but you'll live."

"A goose's egg?" I laughed in spite of my recent injuries. "Maybe next time you decide to tell me I'm in a house where a bunch of girls were murdered, try not to do it on the staircase…in case I flip out.”

Rachel smiled, handing me my flashlight. It had rolled near the front door of the house.

I pressed the button to turn it on, but nothing happened. “Damn,” I muttered. “Maybe this place really is haunted.”

Rachel looked at me with a grave expression. “It’s not haunted. You see, there are some things in life worse than ghosts and monsters…”

“And yeah, what’s that?” I asked, confused.

“Monsters who look like humans. They wear the same form as you and I, but underneath the mask…”

I stared at her silently.

Upstairs, she showed me where they kept the girls. She told me the whole, gruesome story… The story of an evil family who trafficked girls and drugs, a family that’d spawned generations of evil.

“So, that’s why none of the owners rebuilt around here. Nobody wanted to be near this place,” I mumbled softly, staring out one of the girls’ windows. A perfect view of the river, and what used to be the asylum on the other side. I shivered involuntarily.

“So, what’s the carnival want with this place? Why do they set up here on this awful street, with its awful history?” I asked.

“Well for one, they have plenty of room since there aren’t any other houses around. And two, they use this place as a haunted house for Halloween.”

My eyes widened disbelievingly. “That’s the most fucked up thing I’ve heard all day.”

"I know," she said, making her way back toward the stairs.

"Can we sleep in that empty room we came in? I don't like it up here and want to be close to the window or door to get out of this place if we need to," I commented seriously.

"Oh, I told you it's not haunted."

We made our way back downstairs.

"I'm not afraid of ghosts. I'm afraid of the Garretts," I whispered.

Despite my fear, I was so tired and cold that I rolled up in my blanket, scooting close to Rachel since she had the one working light. I wasn't normally the praying type, but I said a few just in case before dozing off.

Chapter Sixteen

"Get up! Get up, Josie! They're here a day early!" Rachel shouted. Instantly aroused from sleep—thinking the heinous Garrett family was back from the dead—I leapt to my feet, gathering up the blanket I'd slept on.

My eyes still full of sleepiness, I stumbled around the room, helping Rachel gather up our snack wrappers and bottles. It was morning time, the sun brightening the empty room and making it considerably less scary than I remembered.

"Who's here?" I whispered, following her as she climbed out the window.

"Shhhh…the carnival workers," she whispered back.

"Oh."

Rachel tip-toed up to the house's edge, peering around the corner of its crumbled exterior. I immediately heard the sounds of tools. Hammers and drills hard at work.

"Do you see Pockets?" I asked, wide awake now.

"No, the carnies aren't here yet, but the setup

crew is. They're assembling the tents on the other side of the house. Act casual, like you're a jogger," she said suddenly, then took off jogging down Clemmons Street.

I stood there, stunned. But then quickly took off behind her.

Jogging forward, I caught a glimpse of the setup crew. They were indeed erecting tents, and farther down the street I could see the disassembled spaceship ride and multiple sets of game booths.

The Carnival de Arcanorum was back in town. Although Rachel said the carnies wouldn't kidnap Freya, after the story last night about the evil families who'd resided in Flocksdale in the past, I felt more certain than ever that something terrible had happened to my friend.

Chapter Seventeen

Finally slowing to a walk, I followed behind Rachel, gasping from the physical exertion. She kept on going, away from the House of Horrors and the carnival on Clemmons Street, which was where I needed to be if I ever wanted to find Freya.

Reaching the heart of Flocksdale, it seemed tiny but trendy with small, eccentric stores and crowds of townspeople coming and going on the sidewalks. There were a few people riding their bikes.

When we finally stopped in front of a rundown drugstore, I took the opportunity to ask what the hell was going on. "I'm supposed to be looking for Pockets at the Carnival de Arcano—or however the fuck you say it, not running in the opposite direction!"

"Whoa…what did you call it? The Carnival of what?" Rachel asked, perplexed.

"The Carnival de Arcanorum," I said, trying my best to pronounce the strange Latin word. "I can look things up too. It means Carnival of Secrets. But why don't you already know this?" I asked, my eyebrows furrowing.

But before she could respond, I was thinking out loud. "The Carnival de Arcanorum..." I said wondrously. "They must change the name from town to town. That's why I couldn't find anything about them on the internet. They're constantly switching names. If it wasn't for your mom's book, I never would have linked the carnival to Flocksdale..." I considered, still rubbing some sleep from my eyes.

Rachel stared at me, hands placed on hips—a defensive stance. "That's stupid. Why would they change the name?"

"Well, what do they call themselves when they come home and set up for the week?"

Rachel stared at me dumbly. "Flocksdale's Carnival. Duh."

"Ever tried to search for 'Flocksdale's Carnival' on the internet?" I pushed.

She shook her head. "No. Why would I? I never even go. Don't want to see my mom showing off her—" Her face reddened.

"So, what now? Why are we running?" I asked.

"I didn't want anyone to see me there. My mom would shit if she knew I stayed overnight in an abandoned house—in the haunted house, no less."

"Wait. You're so damn confusing! You said it wasn't haunted."

"No, but it's about to be. They're going to spend the day setting up the carnival attractions, and the House of Horrors is one of them. They're going to stage it up all scary-like and turn it into the freakiest haunted house in town...although I never go. Like I said, I usually stay home. But look—the setup crew's there, but not the regulars. They'll be there by sundown, I'd guess. We might as well wait, sneak up on Pockets. Maybe Freya's with him. Maybe she ran away and we'll find her when we find him."

I mulled it over. She was right—waiting till all the carnival workers arrived and opened the carnival was probably the best idea. I didn't want to spook Pockets, or Freya, if she was with him. I needed to talk to them both. And the idea that maybe Freya ran away instead of being kidnapped…well, that seemed believable too.

"Well, what the hell are we gonna do until the carnival, then?" I asked Rachel.

She shrugged. "Maybe go eat, then go hang out at the cemetery?"

The cemetery…great. This town was pretty pathetic if its only distractions were an abandoned old house, a cemetery, and a stupid carnival.

***

Although I still felt an inexplicable urgency to locate Freya, my feelings for Rachel and her well-being were of the utmost importance to me. I could tell as the day wore on that she was growing more and more nervous. "Are you worried about going to the carnival?" I asked finally. We were walking around an empty, rundown skating rink. There was nothing much to do but talk.

"I'm just a little anxious, that's all," she said. "Like I said, I haven't been in years and now I'm going with you…"

"Don't worry. We're in it together," I assured her. She smiled brightly, her mood lifting. We'd spent hours killing time in Flocksdale, wandering the streets, our overnight blankets tucked under our arms and Rachel's backpack weighing—and slowing—us down.

"Let's drop off this stuff and go to the carnival," she said finally. We made our way toward Saints Road. I stood outside, down the street, waiting for her to take our belongings inside and come back.

"It's time," she said strangely, heading toward Clemmons Street.

It wasn't long before I heard the loud music and sounds of the crowd. I could see bright lights up ahead—Clemmons Street was no longer deserted.

When we stepped on the midway, I briefly experienced something similar to déjà vu. *No matter where it's at, or what city's it in, this carnival looks just the same*, I thought warily. Rides and booths were lined up, the House of Horrors standing dark and lit up in the distance. Rumbles of recorded haunting sounds emanated from its doors and windows.

"Let's just hope they cleaned up that stupid light that fell," Rachel muttered. I frowned. *What sort of twisted fucks used the actual site of dozens of kidnappings and murders to host a haunted house?* Tomorrow was Halloween and all, but it just didn't seem right. Disrespectful of the dead girls and their families.

They should call it the Carnival of Dead Girls, I thought grimly.

The first thing I did was look around for Evan, the boy from the milk carton game. It didn't take long to find him. He was working the same booth.

Evan's face was half-hidden by a crowd of college-aged boys standing in front of his booth, tossing those impossible rubber balls at the plastic jugs of milk. "Evan!" I shouted. Rachel jumped, clearly unprepared for my shout. *Why was she so edgy?*

Standing on the tips of my toes, I tried to look over the group of boys. Evan saw me right away. A look of confusion crossed his face, but then he broke into a smile and waved affectionately.

"What the heck are you doing here, Josie?" He was wearing a bewildered yet pleased look on his face. And then it occurred to me…he thought I'd come here for him.

Clearing my throat, I got straight to the point. "Where is Pockets?" I asked firmly.

Without asking any questions, but clearly disappointed, Evan pointed in the direction of the Big Top again. I didn't find Pockets there last time, and probably wouldn't this time either. I sighed.

"He's probably behind the Big Top with all those freaks," Evan said. At the mention of the word "freaks," I could feel Rachel stiffen beside me.

"That's my mom you're talking about!" she shouted defiantly. Evan looked from her to me, raising his eyebrows questioningly.

"Lucy is her mom," I explained.

Evan chuckled. "I know. I'm from this town, remember? We all know each other around here."

He and Rachel exchanged death glares.

"Come on." I took Rachel by the hand and led her in the direction of the Big Top. "We'll be back," I called out over my shoulder to Evan.

"No, we won't," Rachel grumbled.

"Sorry about that," I whispered, heading for the big red tent that housed the main show.

"This is why I hate coming here. At school, I get to just be me. But I don't like to be associated with the carnival, or made fun of because of my mom. I don't know why I get so bent out of shape when people call her a freak. I mean, they call *themselves* freaks, right?"

I didn't know how to answer that.

As we went inside the Big Top, I was greeted by the same lady at the front. "I'm looking for my friend, Pockets," I said matter-of-factly, calling him my "friend" so as not to raise any suspicion from the woman.

"He's in the back. The Freak Show tent," she said flatly.

"Are you ready to see your mom?" I asked, catching a glimpse of Rachel's face. I got the sense that she never saw her mother in her work element.

She didn't answer but simply nodded. We walked to the tent behind the Big Top, to the same spot The Freak Show tent was before, in Lamison. I recognized the same blood-red sign from before. Only this time the name had changed, just like the general name of the carnival itself. The sign read **'Flocksdale's Freak Show.'**

"What is up with all the name changing?" I asked again. Rachel just shrugged, chewing her lip anxiously.

"I don't know, but I'll ask my mother when we find her."

"This is it," I said, preparing Rachel, but she surprised me by stepping inside ahead of me.

Last time I was here, I'd been with Evan and didn't need a ticket, so I felt pretty foolish when I saw the man at the front with his top hat and tails.

"I'm sorry. We have to go all the way back out to the midway to get a ticket for the show."

"She's my mom," Rachel said, pushing me forward. "I think the least they can do is let me in here to see her since I'm her daughter."

She stepped up to the man and told him just that. "My mom is the bearded lady," she said matter-of-factly. "I need to see her now."

Instead of looking at her, the man seemed to be staring at me, a strange expression on his face. I wondered if he recognized me from the carnival in Lamison...

"Okay." He lifted the velvet rope aside to allow our entrance to the tent.

"She's right over there." I pointed to the same side where her mom had been standing last time. Rachel was walking so briskly that I had to pick up the pace significantly to keep up with her.

She stumbled right up to her mom's booth. "Mom! Mom, it's me!"

Lucy was surrounded by gawkers just like last time, and when she looked up at the person calling out "Mom," the look on her face was haunting. That proud grin she wore before collapsed on her face. Covering her mouth and beard with her hands, she was obviously shocked to see her daughter.

Lucy's face turned a deep shade of red, obviously embarrassed for her daughter to see her like this. I suddenly realized why Rachel had seemed so nervous. This was nerve-racking for both mother and daughter. I instantly regretted dragging Rachel along with me.

I turned away as they awkwardly embraced and whispered back and forth. I immediately noticed the man in the top hat watching us—specifically me.

Lucy's "exhibit" was surrounded by soft velvet roping, but Rachel had climbed right over it to hug her mom. *With Lucy on the road all the time with the carnival, they probably don't get to see each other much at all*, I realized sadly.

"I've missed you so much, Mom," I heard Rachel saying, a pleading quality to her voice. An unspoken plea for her mother to stop leaving. I thought about my own mother, rotting away in jail. Like Rachel, my mother's whereabouts were embarrassing for me, but at least her mother wasn't a criminal. *Sometimes I wish she'd done something cool, like rob a bank or pull off some heist. But no, she went to jail for her drug problems.*

Lucy called out, "I'm taking a break!" to no one in particular, interrupting my thoughts.

I leaned toward Rachel and whispered, "I'll be back for you in a bit. I'll let you spend time with your mom. Gonna snoop around and ask questions, hopefully run into Pockets…"

She nodded, walking off with her mother to a semi-secluded bench near the far left wall of the freak show tent. Despite her embarrassment over her mom's occupation, Rachel looked happy and at peace. I couldn't help feeling pleased for her. She seemed nice, like someone I could be real friends with…unlike Freya.

But I hadn't forgotten my reasoning for coming back to the carnival. I felt certain that Freya was in danger, and my priority was tracking her down.

I walked around Flocksdale's Freakshow, looking at the same booths from the other day. I spotted the small shack with the dead oddities in it, and the same creep working the door. I moved around the arena, looking from booth to booth, and around the crowd, for any sign of Pockets.

I'd planned on heading back out to the midway, but instead, I approached the man in the shop, a nervous tingle in my step.

"I'm here to see Pockets. Can you find him for me?" I put on my best brave face.

The man looked at me disdainfully, but then said, "Wait right here."

Oddly, he entered the same wooden door in the back of the shack, the one he was guarding last week. Pacing around the booth, I once again looked at the creepy specimens behind glass. *What a weird place*, I thought, eager to get the hell out of there.

"Who the hell are you?" a man called out in a booming voice. I turned around and came face to face with Pockets. Up close, the man was even uglier than he seemed before, with deep fissures, scars, and pus-filled boils on his face. The menacing look on his face didn't help either.

Chapter Eighteen

I wasn't in the mood for exchanging introductions with this scumbag. "Tell me where Freya is," I demanded, glaring at the ugly man named Pockets. He stared at me dumbfounded, but then a momentary spark lit his eye. He rubbed his chin carelessly.

"Who?"

"You know who I'm talking about. The girl you kidnapped from the town you just left, in Lamison Point."

"Whoa! Did you really just say *kidnapped*?" he asked, bringing his hands up in a defensive posture. "I don't know who you are or what you're talking about, little girl, but you're lucky you're not a man or I'd—"

"You'd *what*?" I asked angrily, stepping closer to his face. Only, I had to look up because he was nearly a head taller. Lunging forward, Pockets pulled his arm back, preparing to throw a punch at me. I stood there, stunned.

"Hey!" yelled the man from the stool, coming up

behind Pockets. "Now wait a minute, Pockets. You can't go hitting customers. Or little girls, for that matter. I'm sure there's a rational explanation for this and this girl is simply mistaken." He stared at me with tiny slits for eyes, an expression of sheer disdain.

"Now what are you saying about this man, girl?" he asked, pointing a crooked finger at Pockets.

"My friend, Freya…well, she *was* my friend but not anymore…This man—" I poked a finger at Pockets, "—was the last person to see her before she disappeared. They were kissing on the spaceship ride…what do you call it…Megatron? I know that he knows who I'm talking about!"

My hands on my hips, I wouldn't budge. The man looked at Pockets, raising an eyebrow inquisitively.

"Look, I've been known to kiss lots of stupid girls when I come through town. Ask anyone, and they'll back that up." He chuckled. "I'm sorry I stole your little girlfriend from you, but that's just life," Pockets said, sneering at me evilly.

I thought about the ride spinning around and around, his eyes locked on mine as Freya ridiculed me in his ear…

"I've had lots of girls. I don't recall the one you're talking about. And I sure as hell don't know anybody named Freya," he said flatly. Once animated, now he feigned boredom.

"He's lying," said a voice from behind me. The voice came from Rachel, and she was standing beside me now, chin jutting out defensively.

"I know a liar when I see one," she said

haughtily. Pockets released a loud guffaw.

"And I know a future *freak* when I see one. When's your beard coming in, huh?" He leaned forward and brushed his fingers across her jaw line. "How long do you think you have before you can take your mother's place?"

Those were the last words out of his mouth as I threw a wild punch that landed straight across his jaw. The next thing I knew, Pockets was on top of me and we were rolling around on the dirt floor of the tent, knocking over displays and causing quite an uproar of cheers and boos from the crowd. On top of me now, he gripped my forearms, delivering a painful squeeze. His eyes widened maniacally as he squeezed harder and harder, like a psychotic blood pressure cuff.

Finally, two sets of hands pulled us apart, and I fell back on my butt. I gasped for breath.

Rachel bent down beside me. "Are you okay?" she asked, reaching out to touch the scrapes on my right knuckle.

"I'm fine," I said, jerking away from her. "I'm sorry." I instantly regretted my anger toward her. It wasn't her fault Pockets was such a prick.

"It's okay," she assured me. The two men who broke up the fight were standing across the arena, still attempting to calm Pockets down. "Listen, Josie," she said, "if he knows anything about Freya's whereabouts, he's obviously not going to tell you. I think we need to reevaluate our game plan. For the time being, I think we should get the hell out of here and away from him before somebody decides to call the cops."

"Yeah, on *him*. What kind of guy tries to fight a girl half his size?" I muttered. She pulled me to my feet.

"Meet you back outside the tent. Let me go tell my mom where I'm going first," Rachel said. I followed her instructions, exiting the freak show tent without looking back at that creep, Pockets. *What the hell had Freya seen in that guy? It certainly wasn't his looks or personality.*

A few minutes later, Rachel came strolling out of the tent. I was still high on adrenaline and sheer anger fumes. "I know you want to kick that guy's ass right now, but I think our best bet is to spend some time canvassing the area and asking people questions," Rachel recommended.

Fighting with Pockets wasn't getting me anywhere, and she was right. We headed out to the midway, observing the games and rides. "Do you have a picture of Freya?" Rachel asked. Immediately, I remembered the sketch I'd made on the bus. It was rumpled up in the bottom of my duffel bag, which Rachel had stashed at her home with hers. Not to mention the mess I'd made of her face in the drawing…I dug for my phone in my pocket. I dreaded turning it on because I knew I'd have a million missed calls from home. But the phone contained my only snapshot of Freya.

I turned the phone on, instantly sliding the volume button down on the side. I held out the phone to Rachel. "It's like picture 853 or something…"

We moved through the crowds, stopping at every booth to show the workers and concessionaires

Freya's picture. The first several people we talked to just shook their heads or said no. But a fair-skinned blonde working a skeeball booth said, "Yeah, I saw her! She's that girl that was hanging out with that loser, Pockets. She had some really cool-looking hair. Never seen hair that color before…"

I practically yelled over the girl to get her to stop blabbering. "When did you see her last?" I asked specifically.

"Oh," the girl said, pressing a finger to her temple as she thought it over. I thought about that childish saying, about the brightest crayon in the box…

"I saw her in Lamison, last Wednesday or Thursday, I think."

We thanked her for her help and moved on. "Wednesday and Thursday are the two days that I was there, and I saw her then too," I explained to Rachel. "What I'm trying to figure out is if anyone has seen her since then. In Flocksdale."

The man in the booth next to the talkative skeeball worker put up a hand to stop us. "I want a turn!" he said, his laughter revealing no teeth.

"We're looking for a girl," Rachel said.

"Her name's Freya and she's missing," I explained, holding up the cell phone picture. The old man let out a long whistle.

"Yep. I saw her. She was a fine one, that girl…I saw her just the other day."

"When?" I asked, hopeful of new information.

"I'm not sure." He scratched his beard thoughtfully. "I think it was just a couple days ago.

Yeah…now that I think a little harder, it was just a few days ago. The day before we left to come home."

"So, you saw her the day you were packing up to leave, in Lamison Point?" I prompted. He nodded. "What was she doing when you saw her?"

The man thought about it for a few seconds before answering. "Well, the first time I saw her it was early in the evening 'cause I was setting up my clown targets. She was with that guy that has all those marks on his face. She was walking beside him. I remember looking at him and then looking at her, and I was wondering how he bagged a chick like her."

"And the second time you saw her?" I asked through clenched teeth.

"The second time I saw her she was running," the old man said flatly.

"She was *running*?" I asked, my chest tightening. "Who was she running from?"

He shrugged. "Didn't see anyone chasing her, if that's what ya mean. She was just running. She ran past my booth and kept going until I couldn't see her anymore."

After gaining that strange bit of information, I felt more certain that Freya had been at the carnival right before they skipped town. And obviously trying to get away from someone. Maybe someone who grabbed her and took her away with them…That still brought me back to suspect number one—Pockets.

"I don't know, Josie…that old guy might've been wrong. He seemed a little off kilter." Rachel made circular motions with her finger, indicating he was nutso.

I sighed, feeling frustrated. "I don't want to go back into the freak show tent and have another run-in with Pockets, so maybe, if you don't mind, you can go in there and make the rounds. Ask some of the different people from the exhibits if they've seen her, including your mom," I suggested. I started to hand over the phone with the picture, but then realized I wouldn't have a photo to show while we canvassed separately.

I stopped at a booth, its windows lined with sticky globs of cotton candy and caramel apples. There was a napkin dispenser next to the window and I grabbed a few for myself. "Do you have a pen I could borrow for a sec?" I asked a middle-aged brunette working the booth. She frowned, but passed one to me through the window.

It took me under a minute to sketch a small image of Freya's face with all of its delicate, haunting features.

"She's really pretty," Rachel said, mesmerized. "I can't believe you can draw so well." She studied it for a few minutes, then tucked the drawing in her back pocket. I watched her walk away, heading in the direction of the freak show tent.

I wandered around the park aimlessly, trying to think of anything else I could do to find Freya. *Damn you, Freya. You're always so damn selfish*, I thought. I still felt angry with her for ditching me for a jerk like Pockets and saying such hurtful things. But as much as I didn't want to, I cared for the girl and needed to know she was safe.

If I found her, I didn't expect to be friends again. In fact, I didn't *want* to be her friend anymore. But at the very least, I wanted to find her for her mother. I could only imagine what Filomena was going through. I'd never met Freya's father, but I'd guess he was going through something similar.

Thinking about Freya's family reminded me of my own. I pulled my phone out, staring at the childish smiley face on the cover. My father bought it for me. It was stupid, but I loved him too much not to put the damn thing on and carry it around.

I turned the volume back up, my eyes glazed over as I waited. Instantly, there were hundreds of chimes and dings, alerting me of missed calls, texts, and social media notifications. There were also several voice messages.

I didn't have to read the text messages or listen to the voicemails to know who they were from. Undoubtedly, my dad and Candy. *They must be irate right now*, I thought nervously. More than anything, I could imagine both of them wracked with worry and concern for my well-being. Hell, they probably thought I was kidnapped too.

I found a semi-quiet picnic area before I dialed Candy's number. I don't know why I chose to call her instead of my dad, but it felt like the right choice.

I wasn't ready for her to answer, but she picked up quick, her voice filled with relief. "Josie! Thank God!" she exclaimed. I could hear from the quake in her voice that she'd been crying. Even though I didn't like her much, I had to fight back tears of my own.

"Candy, I'm okay…I promise," I said breathlessly. "I'm so sorry for taking off on you, and I can't tell you where I am, but I want you to know that I'm safe."

Suddenly, I could hear my dad's worried voice in the background. "Please tell Dad I'm fine, and I'm s-sorry," I stammered.

Candy immediately began asking questions—where was I and what was I doing and could they come pick me up?

Pinching my eyes shut, I said, "I'll be back in a few days. Try not to worry too much, Mom." And then I hung up.

While waiting for Rachel to come back, I decided to enter the Big Top to ask more people about Freya. The seats were filling up for the next show, and little kids were in the middle again, awaiting their turn on the animals' backs.

I walked toward the center of the arena. A handful of entertainers were stretching and setting up props for their performances. I pulled up the picture on the phone, strolling up to the lion tamer.

The man was musclebound and shirtless with a posture straight as an arrow. I approached slowly and nonthreateningly so as not to upset the lion standing beside him.

"Hi," I said softly. The man jerked his head in my direction. Slowly, I stuck the picture out toward him.

"Have you seen this girl?" The line was getting extremely old, and the only good information I'd received was from the semi-crazy man in the clown dunk booth.

The man with the lion hesitated just long enough for me to realize he might know something. "What do you know?" I demanded, suddenly unaware of the lion now. The man shook his head.

"Not me. I don't know anything. But she does," he claimed, pointing at the miniature, dainty girl who I recognized as the flying trapeze artist. She was stretching on the tips of her toes, bending her arms in a seemingly inhuman stretch behind her head. "Her name is Georgina. But she can't talk," the lion tamer informed me.

"Can she hear?" I asked, dismayed. The man nodded.

I made my way over to the small, angelic girl. The size of her body made her look similar to a twelve-year-old girl, but as I got closer, I saw the lines on her face clearly marking her as adult.

"Hey, there."

The girl instantly shook her head, placing a hand to her throat, indicating her inability to talk.

"That's okay," I said patiently. "I just want to know what you can tell me about this girl." I handed her the phone, my hand shaking. She looked at the picture, then back up at me. She seemed frustrated, like she had something to say but couldn't.

I felt an equal degree of frustration. But then the trapeze girl stuck up a finger, indicating that she had an idea. She started making an odd motion with two of her fingers, and suddenly I realized she was trying to imitate someone running.

"She was running?"

The girl nodded, smiling.

"Who was she running from?" I pressed, excited to be receiving any type of useful information.

"She was running in here, inside the Big Top?"

The girl pointed at the floor, and then pointed toward the marquee door. I tried to stay calm…and patient.

"She was running out of here?" I asked.

The girl nodded again.

"Do you know *why* she was running? Who did she want to get away from?"

Next, the girl made an ugly expression, poking a finger in small spots all over her face. I understood her meaning completely.

"Pockets," I said, sighing. The girl nodded once again.

I thanked her, heading back to the midway to try to find Rachel. I was more certain now than ever that Freya was here somewhere in Flocksdale, and that she was trying to get away from Pockets. *Maybe she got away*, I wondered hopefully. *Maybe he forced her to come but then she got away somehow. She is pretty feisty*, I considered.

But if she had, why did she not go to the police and report her kidnapping? Something wasn't adding up. And as much as I hated to admit it, something sinister might be going on.

Moments later, I spotted Rachel across the midway, coming out of the freak show tent. She was smiling brightly.

"Okay, I have a plan," she said, pressing her mouth to my ear. "You see all those trailers parked by the river?" I'd noticed them briefly, assuming they belonged to the carnival crew. "Well, my mom stays in her trailer while she's working the carnival, so she's not coming back to the house till next week. My mom called my dad and told him I met a new friend today at the carnival. She's so clueless. She doesn't know who's from around here and who isn't. She's gone traveling too much to care. Anyway, she said we could stay with her in her trailer for a few days, as long as I agreed to help out with the carnival. So, I got to thinking…why don't you try to get some sort of job here? Just temporarily, for a few days…and we can both stay at the trailer."

"That still doesn't help me get any closer to finding Freya," I complained, aggravated.

"Sure it does! During the day we can scope things out and ask questions to see if we can find her. And at night, after the carnival closes and everyone is sleeping, we can sneak out and do some serious investigating. What do you think?"

Her plan seemed crazy. *But it just might work*, I thought hopefully. At this point, I didn't have any better ideas…so it would just have to do for now.

"By the way," Rachel said, "I asked my mom about the carnival changing names from town to town…She acted like it was no big deal. She said they've been doing that, changing the name, for as long as she can remember being with the carnival. She said they often change it from town to town, just like you thought."

"What do you think that means exactly?" I asked, feeling more and more puzzled by this strange place.

"I know my mom isn't involved in anything

bad…but…I definitely think it implies they—or someone working here—has something to hide."

Those were my thoughts exactly.

Chapter Nineteen

"So, who do I talk to around here about getting a job?" I asked, using the sweetest version of my voice I could muster. I was standing in front of Evan's game booth, trying to bat my lashes.

Evan raised his eyebrows. "Seriously? You want to be a carny?" He laughed heartily. "You can't be serious. You don't know the first thing about doing carnival work. Not to be rude, but you'd probably get in the way more than you'd help."

"I may not have experience with carnivals, but I do have a skill," I said, suddenly irritated with this new so-called friend's attitude.

"Oh yeah? What is your skill?" Evan asked, unable to hide his sarcasm. The mocking tone of his voice made me want to punch his lights out.

"This." I held out my sketch book. After forming our plan, Rachel and I had walked to her house to gather our belongings.

Evan opened it up to the drawing of the old house. He squinted at it strangely—not the reaction I was hoping for—but then he started flipping through the other pages. "Damn. These are great, girl. Let's go talk to Malachi about getting you a job drawing people pictures. I think people would pay a pretty penny to get a picture made like one of these."

I couldn't help smiling. Relieved, I followed Evan to meet this guy named Malachi.

"Malachi!" Evan shouted. It was the man with the top hat and he was standing near the freak show tent having a smoke.

"Let me show you what this girl can do." Evan held up the sketch pad, flipping through its pages for Malachi to see.

"Impressive," the man said, but by the tone of his voice he didn't sound too impressed. He took a draw of his cigarette, eyeing me with a creepy smirk.

"Aren't you the young lady who just got into a fist fight with one of my best workers? Why the hell would I want to give a troublemaker like you a job?"

"Because I'll work for cheap, and because I have a talent," I said defensively.

He smiled. "I like your confidence. Okay, I'll give you this job for the week. But I don't want any trouble, you hear?"

I nodded. "Yes, sir." I turned to walk away.

"Wait. I want the picture," he said, pointing at the sketch book. I gave him a confused look.

"Which one?"

"The one of our haunted house," he said pointing at my book and then to the infamous House of Horrors across the midway.

I turned around to look at it, confused. "But it's not—" Staring at the drawing, it did look a lot like the creepy old house we'd stayed in last night. In fact, the resemblance was a little uncanny. Shuddering, I tore the page out and handed it to him. I was glad to get rid of the ugly, evil picture anyway.

Chapter Twenty

My charcoal pencil glided across the canvas effortlessly, taking on a life of its own. When I sketched like this, in my own little world, I never knew what I'd come up with.

I'd never drawn vertically on an easel before, but I felt comfortable doing it this way. Charcoal dust fell easily around me as I focused intently on my subject.

The woman who sat before me was clearly pushing eighty. Her husband stood to the side, tight-jawed, obviously annoyed by this distraction. But the woman sat perfectly still with her hands clasped together on her lap. She wanted the picture to give to her daughter as a present, the old woman explained.

"I've never had my picture drawn, Henry," she'd whined, until finally her husband relented. Considering her age, I suspected that not only would this be her first portrait, but possibly her last.

For that reason, I worked harder than ever, trying to produce something truly majestic for this beautiful, aged woman before me. Despite the damage caused by aging, there was so much beauty in the woman's facial features. Not the sort of "once was" beauty, but a current beauty…a lovely grace she possessed.

Her skin was thin like tissue paper, nearly translucent with its white color and deep blue veins beneath. A cluster of wrinkles surrounded her eyes and streaked her forehead proudly. The cracks around the circumference of her mouth led me to wonder if she'd once been a smoker, and her knobby, scarred hands indicated a life filled with laborious work.

Through my drawing, I could capture it all…

Her smiling, misty-eyed expression when I handed her the drawing made all the hard work worth it. Usually, I hid my drawings from the world, but suddenly, I felt something new—something that felt like pride.

There was nothing in the world that I wanted more than to spend every day of my life doing this—drawing for a living, making people smile.

The woman urged her husband to leave me a generous tip. I accepted the twenty and nodded in thanks, watching the fragile couple move slowly across the midway.

"You're doing quite an impressive job, young lady," said a voice from behind me. It was the man who always wore the coat and hat, the one others called Malachi. Nobody had officially told me, but I suspected that Malachi was the man in charge around here, despite his menial station as a ticket taker of the freak show. There was an air about him, some sense letting me know his position. People respected him, listened to him. Perhaps even *obeyed* him.

"That girlfriend of yours, what's her name?" the man asked unexpectedly. I was about to insist I wasn't a lesbian again when I realized I was just being stupid and insecure.

"Rachel," I answered simply.

"And how does this Rachel know the bearded woman, Lucy?"

My mouth gaped open. All this time, Lucy working for the carnival, and they'd never met her own daughter? *Rachel wasn't lying when she said she never comes to the carnival*, I realized.

"Lucy is her mother." I waited, expecting some sort of explanation for his odd line of questioning, but Malachi offered none.

He moved on, checking in on the other workers in the next booth over. He seemed strange and eccentric, a little intimidating. *But as far as being odd, that description seems to fit most of the workers here*, I thought, chuckling.

Strangely enough, I was sort of enjoying myself. Getting paid to draw for people was an amazing feeling. But I still knew my reasons for coming. I had to investigate Pockets.

According to Evan, I could take breaks whenever I wanted—I simply had to place the **'Be Back Soon'** sign in the window of my booth. I did exactly that, gathering up my bag and heading toward the freak show tent to check in on Rachel. When I found her, she was standing near her mother's tent, chattering amicably with the man who called himself "The Human Pin Cushion." For a moment, I just stood there, silently watching my new friend. Her personality was the exact opposite of Freya's—bubbly and light, always worried about others. Her short blonde hair was pulled back in a stubby little ponytail. She wore little or no makeup. With a face like that, she could bankrupt a whole slew of fancy cosmetic companies.

She smiled when she saw me coming, waving me over to meet her friend—unlike Freya, who never introduced me to anyone. For a brief second, I was struck with sadness. The thought of having to leave Flocksdale, and my new friend, depressed me.

"Hey," I said, shaking hands with "Pinner," which is how Rachel introduced him. He smiled back pleasantly, the piercings on his face stretching painfully. He leaned forward, touching my new ear gauges. With everything going on this week, I'd nearly forgotten about them.

"They're looking a little crusty. Better keep them clean or they'll get infected," he warned. Coming from an expert on needles like him, I made a mental note to clean them really good tonight when I stayed with Rachel.

"Ready for a break?" Rachel asked. We'd been working for hours now and it was nearly one a.m. My belly growled irritably.

We grabbed a couple corndogs and two glass bottles of Coke from one of the concessionaires on the midway, then found a quiet place to sit on a parched strip of grass. We ate our food in silence, both of us hungry since we hadn't eaten anything since lunch.

"I'm ready to give a report. Even though I've been 'working,' I've mostly been watching the workers," she said, using air quotes. "You know, their comings and goings…"

She updated me about Pockets' whereabouts and activities for the past few hours. "I've figured this much out—he spends a lot of time around the Big Top and freak show tent, in and out behind the scenes, but doesn't seem to do anything in particular. Always wearing that smug expression of his…I get the sense he's running errands or taking orders from Malachi, because I saw him 'check in' with him several times each hour. They spoke in hushed voices, looking around nervously each time, like they didn't want to be overheard. And there's another man that checks in regularly with Malachi. I heard someone call him Joseph."

"What does Joseph do around here?" I asked, wondering if I'd seen the man and just didn't know it.

"He seems to be Pockets' right hand man because Pockets and Joseph go back and forth, bringing some heavy props and buckets of material to and from different areas of the carnival. They both check in with Malachi often, but they always do it separately, like they're working in shifts. And here's the thing…there's definitely something going on in that back barn—the one attached to the dead, creepy animal displays."

"I knew there was something fishy going on behind that door!" I exclaimed

"But what that something is, who knows?" she said pensively, taking a sip of her soda. "You don't really think they're holding Freya hostage here, do you?" she asked, a look of horror crossing her face.

"I really hope not," I said, suddenly losing my appetite. "But until I actually see what's in that room for myself, I'll never know."

"Well, let's think this through…If Freya's here, or at the carnival somewhere, we surely would have seen her by now. Don't you agree?"

I nodded. "Yeah, probably…"

"The only way he could hide her here is in his personal trailer or in the back of that room. There's nowhere else she can possibly be without us having seen her by now," Rachel said solemnly. I had to agree.

We sat quietly, each of us considering our options. "So, it sounds like what we need to do is explore Pockets' personal living quarters and find a way to get into that backroom," Rachel said finally. "I think I can come up with a plan," she added, still deep in thought.

I don't know why, but I trusted her. And I knew she'd help me find out the truth about Freya's disappearance. One way or another.

Chapter Twenty-One

Lucy's trailer was small and compact, but neatly decorated and well cared for. It consisted of a tiny kitchenette, living room space, one bathroom, and one bedroom. Just enough space for one person while on the road.

Rachel and I were temporarily camped out in her living room. Despite the late night hour, Lucy cooked for us when we finished up with the carnival—pan-seared chicken, string beans, and applesauce straight from the jar. I was so hungry I would have eaten anything.

The first time I'd met her—at home, in Lamison—I'd felt sorry for her because of her condition. But watching her smiling face as she glided around the kitchen and chatted with her daughter, I saw her for who she was—a normal, happy person.

The lighting in the trailer was dim, so we ate by candlelight at the tiny foldout table that sat in the middle of the floor, between the kitchen and living room. It wasn't the kind of meal I'd expected to eat in a small trailer in the middle of a meadow, right behind a creepy carnival and next door to a real-life House of Horrors.

But I enjoyed the meal and company immensely. And I didn't feel a bit tired.

"What is your condition called?" I asked, immediately feeling rude and foolish for blurting out such a personal question. But Lucy didn't seem to mind one bit.

"It's called 'pogoniasis,'" she explained. "It's caused by an excess of androgens, which are a type of hormone. My mother and her mother both had the same condition. I usually shave when I'm not on the road, so Rachel isn't used to seeing me like this," she said, smiling sheepishly at her daughter.

Lucy went on to describe the difficulties that she faced throughout her childhood because of her condition. The woman had overcome a great deal of adversity in her life, and I couldn't help admiring her for it.

"Kids these days try so hard to be different so they can stand out. Well, I never had that problem. I just used it to my advantage instead of letting it get me down." I couldn't help thinking about my recent trip to the piercing salon and changing my clothes to look different for Freya. *Maybe I just need to start learning to be happy with who I am, like Lucy,* I considered thoughtfully.

After sharing supper and taking turns in the shower, Lucy headed off to sleep in her own bedroom, and the two of us took a seat on the floor in the living room. Rachel sat in a strange Indian-style position that I couldn't imitate even if I wanted to. I sat down on the sofa, noting the time. It was nearly 2:30 a.m.

"Your mom is amazing," I said, smiling at Rachel. "I know you don't see her often, but you're lucky to have her." I couldn't help thinking of my own mom, trying to imagine the contours of her face. Her lopsided grin. Her goofy pranks, chasing me through the house, having spoon fights…

"Okay, I have a plan," Rachel said, getting straight to business.

"I'm all ears," I said, forgetting my mom.

"Tonight," she said seriously, "we're going to check out the living quarters of our fellow carnies, especially Pockets and that crony of his, Joseph. Hopefully, we'll be able to discover something about Freya. But at the very least, we can try to learn something about the key." I stared at her, baffled.

"What key?" I asked, perplexed.

"The key to the back barn of the freak show, of course," she answered, looking pleased with herself. "I watched that door like a hawk, especially toward the end of the night. There is a man who sits on a stool, and his only job is to manage the novelty store, and to make sure that no one tries to go into that room in the back—unless that person is one of three people: Malachi, Joseph, or Pockets. As the evening was closing out, I saw Pockets leave, and then Malachi and Joseph came up behind him and locked it tight with one of those silver skeleton keys. The key was attached to a long silver keychain with one of those hooks that attaches to your pants pocket. I'm pretty sure I saw a similar key around Malachi's neck."

"You're not really suggesting we break into Malachi's house and slip the key out of his pocket, are you?" My stomach instantly filled with nervous jitters.

"Hell no. I'm not that crazy! But we do need to find out where they keep it at night. Because if it's on their necks all day long at the carnival, our only hope of getting to it is when they're passed out. Let's hope they hang it up somewhere or stick it somewhere we can gain access to."

I couldn't help but laugh. She sounded like a natural sleuth.

I was surprised to hear myself say, "Let's do it!"

Chapter Twenty-Two

We waited until it was good and dark before quietly slipping out of Lucy's trailer. Dressed in our blackest clothes, we crept through the dew-laden grass, looking around for people. The House of Horrors was dark. Moonlight danced across the surface of the river.

There were nearly two dozen trailers dotting the empty lots beside the old house. Vendors had covered their booths with plastic and cloth tarps, and rides sat eerily silent.

Rachel carried only her backpack, which she strapped tightly to her back. It contained a few meaningless items, but most importantly, the Maglites and more snacks. "In case it turns into a long night and we get hungry," she'd explained when I looked at the pack crazily.

The living quarters consisted of approximately twenty trailers scattered across a five-acre field behind the carnival. "How the hell are we going to know whose trailer is whose?" I asked, overwhelmed by the number of trailers sitting around us.

"Well, we won't, at least not exactly," Rachel said solemnly. "But…and you can thank me for this later, I asked my mom a few innocent-sounding questions today about which trailers some of her co-workers lived in, so I have an idea about some of them."

I smiled, relieved. *Rachel was so quick-witted and wonderful*, I thought admirably. *And beautiful.*

"You are a diabolical genius, you know that?" I whispered, grinning from ear to ear.

"Let's just see how this goes first, and then you can fawn over me afterwards," she said, returning my smile.

"According to my mom, Malachi's trailer sits on the far west corner, over near the tree line. He is farthest away from us, so we will hit his place last. Pockets and some of the other guys share a trailer, and according to Mom, they're a few doors down from Malachi. Joseph shares a trailer with his wife and son, and they are located on the corner closest to the back end of the freak show tent. I say we head that way first. As far as the other people…I stopped paying attention to what she said after that," she said apologetically.

"Let's head in that direction, but I also say we peek in as many windows as we can along the way, just in case Freya is hiding out in one of them," she added smartly.

I nodded my consent, moving forward wordlessly. I placed a finger to my lips, reminding her that as we approached we had to stay silent.

We stayed at a steady, even pace, not wanting to draw attention to ourselves in case someone was watching. Rachel walked with a delicacy in her step, soft and light like a ballerina. I tried my best to mimic her actions.

The first trailer we came upon was dark, with only one small light shining through the kitchen window area. Rachel was too short to reach the windowsill, which was fine by me because I'd prefer to be the one to get caught if it came down to that.

I crept silently to the edge of the sill, leaning up on the tips of my toes to peer in. The inside layout on this trailer was nearly identical to Lucy's. I immediately saw three men stretched out sleeping on the living room floor, blanket and pillows spread out beneath them. I recognized their faces—the Ferris wheel and bumper car operators. I pointed a finger, signaling to Rachel we should move onward to the next trailer.

We snuck past five more trailers on the way to the one Rachel thought belonged to Joseph and his family. The first three contained sleeping concessionaires, and the last two were too dark to see anything at all.

"I think that's his." Rachel pointed ahead to a rundown trailer on the corner of the back end of the freak show tent. There were a couple lights shining from the trailer, and I hesitated nervously as we got close.

Inching up to the living room window, I tentatively peered through a pair of slotted blinds. I jumped back instantly, startled. The last person I'd expected to see was Evan. In fact, the location of his trailer never even crossed my mind before we started searching. But there he was, curled up sleeping on a twin-sized bed.

I squatted down next to the trailer. I signaled for Rachel to do the same.

"I think Joseph is Evan's dad," I softly whispered. Her eyes widened.

A plan was suddenly beginning to form in my mind. I didn't necessarily like the plan, but it might be our only option at this point.

Signaling again for her to follow me, we slunk along the grassy meadow to the far west corner where Pockets' and Malachi's trailer supposedly sat. First, we slipped up to Pockets' fully darkened windows.

The pale glow of the moon illuminated the ugly contours of Pockets' scarred face. He was—thankfully—sleeping like the dead. For the first time, it occurred to me that he must have been inside one of the houses when it caught fire a few years ago, and that's how he earned his scars. I remembered the story Rachel told me, about the girls trying to burn down the town…

I darted around to the other side of the trailer, peering into the living room and kitchen area windows. Besides Pockets in the bed, the trailer was completely empty. *If Freya's hiding out, she's not doing it in Pockets' trailer*, I realized, disappointed.

Next, Rachel and I made our way toward the last trailer for inspection. The tip of my sneaker got snagged in some sort of animal hole and I fell face first in the grass. "Ugh…" Rachel helped me up, shushing me in my ear. My knee ached fiercely.

Staring ahead at the final trailer, it looked oddly darker than the rest and more decrepit. I didn't hold out much hope that I'd be able to see anything since it was completely cloaked in blackness, but I shimmied up to the front kitchen window and attempted to take a look inside.

"What on Earth are you doing out there, girl?" yelled Malachi, throwing open the trailer door with a bang. Heavy, untied work boots stomped onto the porch.

But the only thing I saw was the high-powered pistol in his hand.

Chapter Twenty-Three

"U-ummm…" I stammered, not knowing what to say to this menacing-looking man with a gun. Thank God Rachel was there to help me out, as usual.

"Sir," she said, raising her hands unthreateningly. "I'm sorry we disturbed you. We were just looking to see if you were awake before knocking because we didn't want to wake you up."

Malachi made a hurry up motion with his hands. I could literally hear both of our hearts beating as we stood helpless at the end of his gun.

"We were wondering if we could talk to you about making our current positions with the carnival permanent. We've enjoyed working here and we'd really like to stick around, if that's all right with you…" Rachel lied.

"Well, creeping around my house at two in the morning is not the way to get yourself a job, missy!" he scolded her. But then he smiled slightly and said, "Okay. You and the other one—you can stay on."

He pointed an accusatory finger at me. "No fighting. No shit-starting, in general. Ya got it?" I swallowed a lump in my throat, barely understanding his words. I was just happy to see the barrel of the gun drop.

I nodded solemnly. Then we both darted off, running back to Lucy's trailer as fast as we possibly could. Once inside, I could finally breathe again.

"Whew! That was a close call." Rachel plopped down on the floor next to the couch. I sank into the cushions, removing my shoes. I was still a little shocked by the gun.

"It's okay," she assured me, reaching out to touch my leg. "We made it out of there without getting shot at least, right?"

I nodded, placing my hand on top of hers.

"Well, I don't think we got too much accomplished tonight," she said, sighing loudly.

"Sure we did." She stared at me, waiting. I smiled. "You're not the only genius around these parts," I teased.

Surprised, she squeezed my hand as hard as she could and demanded, "What did you figure out?"

"If Evan is Joseph's son, and Joseph has a key, all I have to do is find a way to get Evan to take me back to his house. I don't exactly know how I'll get a hold of the key once I get inside, or how I'll talk my way inside in the first place, but it's worth a shot, don't you think?"

Rachel's eyes widened. "That is the best idea we've had so far," she said. "Now let's get some sleep."

We unrolled two sleeping bags her mother had left out for us. I stretched out on mine and Rachel on hers. After an hour of fidgeting, she finally rolled to her side, facing away from me. Gently, I draped my arm over her, enjoying the smell of her hair.

Chapter Twenty-Four

I tracked down Evan on my lunch break. "Hey, man! You want to grab a bite to eat with me for lunch?" I asked, leaning up against the booth where Evan stood, counting out a stack of dollar bills from the milk toss game.

"I thought you'd be eating lunch with your girlfriend," Evan said, not looking up from the wad of bills. I could hear the bitterness in his tone, but for now I chose to ignore it.

"Honestly, that girl is kind of getting on my nerves."

Evan looked up, suddenly interested in this change of topic. But then, trying to play it cool, he shrugged and looked back down at his bills.

"Yeah, I was wondering when you'd get sick of that chick. She seems like she can be pretty damn annoying, if you ask me. Do you think she'll grow a beard like her mom someday?" Evan asked, throwing back his narcissistic head as he chuckled.

It took every bit of willpower I had not to punch this asshole. But remembering the plan I'd discussed with Rachel, I said, "No, I hadn't thought of that. But that's a really good point, Evan." He smiled, pleased with himself for making such a noteworthy observation. *Fucking dick*, I thought, clenching my teeth.

We shared chili cheese fries and pork chop sandwiches at a shaded picnic table caddy corner to the Big Top. "Isn't it nice not having to deal with all that chatter while you eat? That Rachel girl…she seems loud and obnoxious." Evan stuffed his face with fries.

She didn't seem that way at all to me. *I could deal without all of your stupid chatter, Evan,* I thought, biting my tongue.

"You want to hang out tonight when you get off work? Maybe ride a few rides or check out that freak show again? I really want to get a closer look at that six legged horse," I said, pushing my fry basket aside. The look on Evan's face clearly revealed his excitement. I wondered if he thought I liked him. *Ugh.*

"Sure. But what about Rachel?" he asked skeptically.

"Screw her," I said. I stood up and walked away.

***

When darkness fell, I stuck the closed sign on the front of my booth and made my way over to Evan's game station.

"Just finishing up!" Moments later, he was by

my side. "So, what do you want to do first?" he asked eagerly.

I fought the urge to say, *Kick you in the face.*

"How about the freak tent?" I suggested instead. Evan looked more than happy to follow me there.

I made a beeline for the two-headed cat display, but my only real focus was the locked door in the back. The man on the stool still sat at his post. From what I could see, nobody else was around.

"What's in that room?" I asked bluntly, turning to look at Evan. Evan shrugged. "Just a bunch of supplies. Nothing of any real importance in there."

I felt disappointed, not getting more information out of him.

"Let's go check it out," I dared.

"Nah. My uh…Dad keeps it locked up tight because it's full of expensive supplies. He carries that key in his pocket with him everywhere he goes. He'd kill me if he caught me snooping around in there," Evan explained, his cheeks reddening slightly. I realized then that he was afraid of his dad, and his claim that there was nothing important inside was a lie.

Deciding it was pointless to continue pursuing this topic, I changed the subject. "Let's go see those conjoined twins again."

As we made our way over to the Siamese twin exhibit, I immediately spotted Rachel. She was walking toward us, a pissed off expression on her face. She stopped in front of me, hands poised on her hips. She didn't look happy, to say the least.

"What the hell?" she said, throwing up her hands in disgust. "I thought we were supposed to hang out tonight! Why are you with *him*?" she asked, pointing at Evan. The two rivals shared a look of utter disdain.

"Hey! Evan is my friend and I can hang out with him any time I want!"

"Oh yeah? Well, find yourself somewhere else to crash tonight then, because I don't want you sleeping over at my mom's with me."

As Rachel strutted away, I tried not to smile.

Evan, unsurprisingly, was amused by this encounter. "No worries, Josie. You can stay with me at my mom and dad's tonight. In fact, you can stay with us as long as you need to. I'm sure they won't mind."

"Really? You'd do that for me?" I stared at him innocently.

"Sure. What are friends for?"

As we made our way toward more freak show exhibits, I couldn't help feeling excited. Our plan— Rachel's and mine—had been pulled off flawlessly.

Chapter Twenty-Five

At the end of the night, I followed Evan back to his trailer. His mom and dad were already there waiting for their son. I nervously wrung my hands as he introduced me. I'd seen Joseph around the carnival plenty, but his mom didn't look familiar.

"I'm Anita," she said, shaking my hand cordially. She seemed like a jovial lady, soft spoken and kind. Joseph narrowed his eyes at me, but said nothing.

I thought they might object to me staying the night, which would totally mess up my plans, but they seemed perfectly okay with the arrangement. Unlike Lucy's trailer, Evan's trailer had two bedrooms.

I was a little surprised when Evan led me to his room. No way would my dad or Candy let a boy sleep all night in my room. But then Anita called after us, "No hankie pankie, you two! Use your pull-out cot, Evan."

Evan's room looked like a perfectly normal bedroom for a teenage boy. I'd caught a peek of it through his window last night, but it'd been too dark to see much. Childish posters, an unmade bed, and a crumpled stack of pants and t-shirts he'd yet to put away decorated the room. I perched on the side of his bed, sighing.

Two hours later, after showing me his entire collection of baseball cards and comic books. I was bored to tears. But I played the role of dutiful friend flawlessly, asking questions and smiling, all the while irritated on the inside.

After cards and books was movies. Midway through the second film, Evan finally fell asleep on his twin-sized cot. The silence in the trailer was deafening. Although this is what I'd been waiting for, I felt frightened.

Looking over at Evan again, I wanted to be totally sure he was, in fact, sound asleep. I waited nearly an hour before I slowly pushed the covers aside, standing up as quietly as possible. The floorboards slightly creaked, but not enough to wake anyone up—or so I hoped.

I decided that my first course of action would be a trip to the bathroom down the hall, that way I could scope out the house and make sure Joseph and Anita were actually asleep.

Tip-toeing out of Evan's bedroom and through the hallway slowly, I soundlessly slipped into the bathroom. Beyond the bathroom was the kitchen and living room space, and beyond those spaces, Joseph and Anita's bedroom in the back.

I closed the bathroom door and sat on the toilet,

taking in several deep breaths. I ran my fingers through my hair nervously. *If they wake up, all I have to do is say I was thirsty and looking for a glass of water when I wandered into the wrong room.*

I crept back out of the bathroom and made my way to the kitchen. There was a dull light shining over the kitchen sink, illuminating the entire space. My eyes were immediately drawn to a key rack nailed to the side of the kitchen cabinets. I scanned the rows of keys for the silver skeleton key Rachel had described in detail, my heart rate quickening.

Nothing. A few of them were obviously car or house keys, but nothing like she'd described.

Finally working up the nerve to move forward, I tip-toed across the living room. There was a short hallway leading to the master bedroom, and from there I could see the bedroom door was wide open.

I pressed my back against the wall in the hallway. I took a breath then edged my way closer to their door, all the while trying not to make a sound. If I got caught now, there wasn't a whole lot of excuses for sneaking around outside their bedroom.

It was now or never. I did a mental three-count then dropped to the floor, army-crawling my way through the door of the bedroom. And then I heard something move.

I froze, my heart literally stopped beating inside my chest. Someone was rustling around in the bed…

But then as I listened, I heard the pair snoring. *They must have just been moving around a bit in their sleep*, I tried to reassure myself.

I kept moving, using my elbows to guide me along the threadbare carpet.

As I got closer, I stole a glance up at the bed. Joseph was sleeping on the side nearest me. *Thank God for small miracles*, I thought breathlessly. Now I just had to hold out hope that the man didn't wear his jeans to bed, or hide the key elsewhere before going to sleep.

I knew that if he was anything like my dad, he'd just take off his jeans and leave them lying on the floor by the bed.

Jackpot! Miraculously, a faded pair of blue jeans and a button-up shirt were lying on the floor at the foot of the bed. I crawled over to them as quickly and quietly as possible. Pausing, I listened for any sounds that might indicate one of them was waking up.

All was quiet. I slid my hand into the right side pocket of the jeans. Nothing.

I fought back the urge to scream obscenities. Saying a silent prayer, I pulled the jeans closer, slipping my hand inside the other pocket.

My fingertips were rewarded by a small, cold, metal object. I had it!

I held the key tightly in my palm, enjoying the feel of its shiny greatness, and then crawled back out the same way I came in. Hurriedly, I stumbled my way toward the front door and opened it as quietly as possible.

As soon as the crisp October air met my face, I pushed the door closed and took off running, away from Evan's trailer. The key felt great in my palm, like my first real victory since arriving in Flocksdale.

Chapter Twenty-Six

Rachel looked beautiful as she slept. So beautiful, in fact, it nearly pained me to wake her up. I leaned down slowly over her curled up body, gently nudging until her eyes popped open. As soon as she saw it was me, she jumped up expectantly, eager to hear what had happened.

Before she could ask, I said, "I got the key."

"Yay!" I shushed her, afraid of waking up her mom, who was just a room away. Rachel stood up, quickly stripping out of her pajama bottoms and looking around for her jeans.

I reached over to pick them up off of the floor and hand them to her. The sight of her short, tan legs and curvaceous bottom left me grasping for words. I instantly turned around, waiting for her to finish dressing in private. "I don't think we should go now," I said.

"Why not?" She furrowed her eyebrows quizzically, turning me around to face her.

"Listen. I *want* to go now too. But take a look outside your window. The sun will be up in about an hour and everyone will be waking up and heading to work at the carnival," I explained.

"Well, then we don't have much time to spare…Let's go!" she hissed, tugging on my sleeve.

Chapter Twenty-Seven

As soon as we stepped outside, I had to fight the urge to run back in. This seemed way too risky.

The House of Horrors sat still in the distance, mocking us.

Rachel slipped her hand in mine. Slowly and silently, we wound our way through the scattering of trailers. It was nearly five o'clock in the morning, the carnival grounds as quiet as a graveyard. The carnival at night was creepy, with its statuesque rides and abandoned game booths.

Thankful to be out of sight of the workers' trailers, we cautiously slipped inside the freak show tent. Rachel pulled out a small flashlight from her pocket and used it to illuminate the area inside the tent.

Shining the light from side to side, I saw that we were—thank God—alone.

"This way," I said, heading straight for the novelty shack in the back. The man who usually worked the shop was gone for once, and the creepy displays were covered with plastic tarps.

Nervously, I pulled the key out from my pocket and paused next to Rachel in the doorway. "You ready?" I asked in a whispery voice.

She answered by leaning over to kiss my cheek. She nodded. It was time to see what Flocksdale's Carnival—or whatever they called it, considering they changed the name so much—was hiding. I slipped the delicate key into the hole, opening the door to the secret back room.

Chapter Twenty-Eight

Rachel shined the light inside, illuminating the inside of a massive barn. My mouth fell open in shock.

I don't know what I was expecting to find. Freya's dead body? Chopped up animal parts? Thankfully, this wasn't as bad…but this was pretty fucking bad.

There were dozens of metal slab tables, covered with cleaning products, beakers, soda bottles, and coffee filters. I counted five or six metal cauldrons as tall as the tables they stood beside.

An overpowering smell of ammonia filled the air, mixed with a half dozen other chemicals.

"What the hell is this?" Rachel wondered, her mouth open wide to match mine.

"It's a meth lab," I said, stepping further into the room.

I noticed racks of heavy artillery on the back walls.

"A *traveling* carnival meth lab…" I said incredulously.

"Well, at least we know their reason for hiding now. They change their name in case someone's on to them. By the time they figure it out, they're long gone, with a brand new identity in a new small town they can rip apart by saturating it with drugs," Rachel breathed, touching the top of one of the beakers.

"Don't touch anything!" I hissed. "We need to get out of here. *Now.* I can't believe they don't have someone guarding this place overnight. What idiots! But we need to go. If they catch us, they might just kill us."

Rachel and I exchanged worried glances.

"Do you think that's what happened to Freya? Maybe she found out about the drugs while she was hanging around with Pockets, and so he—or somebody—killed her?"

I shook my head back and forth. I didn't want to believe it, but I had to admit it seemed possible.

"Time to go. Now," I said again, pushing her back outside. We locked the room behind us and went back through the entrance of the freak show tent.

The sun was coming up.

Chapter Twenty-Nine

Safely back inside Lucy's trailer, I collapsed on the couch. I felt mentally and physically drained. I hadn't slept all night, and now it was time to go sketch strangers' faces in my booth all day.

"Happy Halloween," Rachel said dully, looking a little peaked herself. "What are we going to do? I mean, they're obviously running drugs all over the U.S. We should just go to the police…"

Rubbing the sleep—or lack thereof—from my eyes, I said, "Just let me think, okay?" I tried to run my fingers through my hair but it was filled with tangles. I touched my new ear piercings. Winced. They were definitely infected.

"First of all, I don't trust the police in this town. No offense, but after all the shit you told me about Flocksdale the other day…I don't trust anyone around here. Well, except you, of course. And your mom…"

Rachel narrowed her eyes at me, but then her face softened. "No, you're right. But if we can't go to the police, where can we go?" I don't know why, but the first person I thought of was Miss Hamm, Lamison's local librarian. She'd know what to do. My dad and Candy would too. We could go to the local police and tell them everything. Maybe with a full investigation, they could prosecute the carnival workers involved in the drug trafficking and press them to tell us where Freya went.

I considered Rachel's words earlier…Maybe Freya *had* found out about the drugs and because of it, they silenced her somehow…

Oh, come on now! I chastised myself. I wasn't a kindergartener. By "silence," I meant they *killed* her.

My hands shook so hard I had to hold them together to make them stop. Rachel was staring at me, chewing her lip. She didn't know what to do either.

"I'll call my dad and Candy tonight. Tell them to come out here. I'm afraid if I leave and go home, the carnival will take off from Flocksdale and then the cops will never be able to track them down. I need to be here—watching to make sure these assholes don't go anywhere, while we wait for help to arrive," I said finally. I was glad to have some sort of plan.

"Well, for now I'm going to go over and work at the carnival, like I'm supposed to. If I can, I'll try to take a few pics with my cell phone—get proof of who's coming and going from that back room." I stood up, gathering my pencils and stuff for my booth.

"No, not you. You need to sleep for a couple

hours. I'll tell my mom and Malachi you're sick. Mom will be up any second now, so make sure you play sick."

"No way," I protested, shaking my head back and forth. The thought of leaving her alone at the carnival with those creeps…

"I'll stay with Mom the entire time. And I'll be back in three hours to wake you up. And I won't take no for an answer."

To be honest, I was too damn tired to argue. I lay down on the couch. My legs were so long I had to prop them up on the arm rest, but it didn't matter…I was out within minutes, a dreamless sort of sleep.

Chapter Thirty

When I opened my eyes, I was surrounded by darkness—pitch black, panic-inducing darkness. I leapt to my feet. *What the hell?*

It took me a minute to gather my senses, remembering I was staying at Rachel's mom's trailer on the carnival grounds in Flocksdale. "Why's it so dark in here?" I muttered, stumbling around what I hoped was the living room I'd slept in.

My knee banged against some piece of furniture with a sharp edge. *Probably a coffee table,* I thought, biting my lip to distract from the knee pain. Using my hands to guide me, I stepped forward slowly, fumbling around in the dark, groping for something, anything. Blessedly, the tips of my fingers grazed the wall.

I followed it until I found the familiar form of a light switch. When the lights came on, I let out a sigh of relief. Lucy's trailer stood quiet, empty.

I went to the kitchen, opening the blinds to look out. As I suspected, it was nighttime. The carnival was booming. Flashes of green, red, and yellow blinding me. *Why the hell did Rachel let me sleep so long?* I thought angrily.

Unzipping my bag, I got out a change of clothes and tied my hair up in a bun. I dressed quickly, used the bathroom, and found some toothpaste to brush my teeth. I turned my phone on to check the time.

Like yesterday, my phone lit up with missed messages and texts. I immediately saw a text from my dad.

Dad: Josie, please come home! I'm worried sick.

And then I saw several more, a few of them from Dad and two from Candy.

Candy: I'm sorry that I can't be like your real mom. But I do love you and I want to be close with you. Please, just tell me where you are and we will come get you. You're not in trouble. I just want you home. Please...

Candy: Josie, sweetie...please call or text me back. Your dad has been losing his mind and the police are out looking for you. Tell me where you are and I'll come get you. We'll figure this out together, me and you, as friends...

Candy: I love you, Josie. I love you so much. Please be okay...

My eyes welled up with tears, my stomach churning with guilt. *How could I have done this to them? I'm going to fix this now. I'm going to tell them where I am so they can come and help me figure out what to do about Flocksdale and Freya and this entire mess...*

I stared at the phone. My text message box held one more message. I wasn't ready to read another message from my parents, but I clicked to open it anyway. I was so surprised by what I read that I dropped the phone to the floor.

Horrified, with my hand over my mouth, I reached over and picked up the phone. The message was from Freya.

Freya: Hey there, stranger! Pockets told me you came searching for me. I guess you know our secret...I decided to join the carnival LOL. Fuck my parents. And fuck that lame ass town of Lamison. I can't believe you came all this way. Please don't tell my parents I'm here. I don't want to go back there.

I immediately started texting back...

Me: Oh my god, Freya. I'm just glad you're okay. Where are you? I was so scared.

Minutes went by and I started wondering if— once again—I'd never hear from her. I sat down on the sofa again, staring at the phone. Willing a text to come through.

And then it did.

Freya: I'm here, silly! Like I said, I'm in Flocksdale. I've been hiding out, but since you already know and I know you won't tell my parents, I might as well have some fun. I'm getting ready to go inside the haunted house.

I dropped the phone, forgetting all about my plans to call home. I jammed my shoes on my feet and took off running. Straight toward the House of Horrors.

Chapter Thirty-One

There were kids in costumes everywhere. If they'd been dressed like normal, I probably would have forgotten the holiday. I darted through a sea of vampires and witches, girls dressed like hookers and boys with Jason masks.

I was shocked to see the House of Horrors, still dark and mysterious, but now lit up and busy—with a creepy cemetery scene in the front, fog machines, and more ghostly sounds booming from a set of speakers. The haunted house was in full swing tonight.

Distant screams filled my heart with dread, but I darted up the concrete driveway. The front door was open, no ticket taker in sight. I stepped inside the foyer. It was pitch black like the other day, only this time there were shrieks coming from other rooms, annoyingly scratchy cobwebs everywhere, and a plastic cackling skeleton.

"Freya!" I shouted uselessly in the dark.

"Freya, Freya…" a squeaky girl's voice mocked me, somewhere off the kitchen. I followed the sounds, my heart nearly stopping as I spotted strobe lights ahead.

"Welcome to the House of Horrors," a deep male voice spoke in my ear. I nearly jumped out of my own skin. Like Malachi, he was wearing a top hat and tails, but this guy was younger. Scruffier.

"I'll be your guide," he said, holding out an old-fashioned candle on a tray to guide us.

Oh, I get it. This is one of those haunted houses where you have a creepy tour guide who makes sure you don't punch the attractions or get lost in the dark and sue.

There were several plastic dolls, dirty and eyeless, lined up on chairs in the foyer. A few small, creepy animatronics, but nothing over the top.

"This way, please!" the guide insisted, waving me toward the stairs. I could see now with the glow from his candle.

"This doesn't seem very scary," I remarked, placing my foot on the first stair. He followed behind me, urging me up the stairs.

"Freya!" I shouted again. "Freya, it's Josie! If you're in here, come find me! Please!" My voice sounded more desperate than I would have liked.

"Pick a room…any room," my guide said as we reached the top of the stairs.

"It doesn't matter which you choose, you'll be doomed any way you go…" he added.

I frowned. This was stupid. Freya wasn't inside, obviously. I listened for more screams or squeals in the dark, but heard nothing. It was eerily silent up here on the second floor.

"Where do I go?" I asked impatiently. "I just want to get out of here. I'm looking for a friend."

"How about the first room?" the creepy butler suggested. He was blocking my path to the stairway. Instead of taking his suggestion, I selected the second doorway. There appeared to be approximately eight rooms upstairs, all of the doors closed tightly. No sounds emanating from any of them.

Suddenly feeling nervous, I stepped back from the door, removing my hand. "I don't want to do this. I'm going back outside to look for my friend."

I tried to weave my way around him in the hall, but he moved side to side, blocking me.

"Seriously, fucker. I'm going to scream as loud as I can if you don't fucking move. I'll tell them you're trying to rape me!"

He smiled strangely. "Pick a door, any door…" he repeated, his voice even and calm.

"Help! He won't let me out of here!" I shouted angrily, my voice hoarse and prickly. Panic was rising in my chest. I didn't like being in here and I didn't like this fucking creep. And I didn't like the fact that it was so damn quiet in here all of a sudden.

"Pick a door, before it picks you," he said, stepping close to me in the dark. His face was inches away from mine now. I felt my blood run cold.

I was going to have to shove him and run for dear life. But before I had the chance, I heard one of the bedroom doors behind me open and close. I whipped around, locking eyes with a demented clown standing at the end of the far hallway.

He was wearing a dirty yellow clown costume, with exaggerated footwear and bright white makeup. But this was no slapstick clown. Nearly six feet tall, he stared at me, his head tilted to the side crazily. There was something red all over his face.

I turned to fight off the butler instead, but when I did, he quickly blew out the candle. I shrieked. Now I was in the dark with the butler and clown.

Chapter Thirty-Two

I reacted quickly, reaching for the knob to the second door in the dark. I darted inside the room, slamming the door behind me. *It's just a haunted house. This isn't real. Not real, not real, not real…*I repeated over and over.

"Lock the door," whispered a girl's voice from behind me. Without looking back, I did, fumbling for the lock mechanism in the dark.

But it wasn't dark, not completely. Dull lights flickered. *Trick lights, like strobes,* I realized.

I looked around the room for the girl. Not seeing her, I turned back to the door. I pressed my ear against it, listening.

I couldn't hear anyone coming.

"Over here," the voice said again. That's when I saw where the voice was coming from. A frail girl, younger than me, was chained to a radiator in the far left corner. The dim lights barely illuminated her face, but I could see that she wore a scared expression.

I ran over to her, nearly tripping over a curled up rug on the floor. We were in a tiny bedroom, no more than fourteen feet by twelve feet. A small window let in a pale strip of light.

I crept forward, falling to my knees beside her. Pale and blonde, her eyes were sunken and lifeless. *Nice makeup*, I thought, rolling my eyes.

But then I saw a large bruise on her arm. And shoulder. And the other side of her cheek. The bruises were bulging and purple.

"What the hell? This isn't funny anymore," I said, backing up and away from the girl.

"They kidnapped me. Stole me from my family. They did…horrible things to me," she whined, staring at me, unblinking.

"I want out of here," I begged. "I'm looking for my friend and I want out. Is there some sort of emergency exit around here? Seriously, I could sue you for not letting me out…" I warned, trying to swallow but unable to.

"The only way out is the trap door," she whispered hoarsely.

"What trap door?" I looked around the room confusedly.

Lifting her shackled hands, she pointed across the room. Sure enough, in the flickering lights, I could see a tiny square panel on the wall. The space was barely large enough to crawl through.

"Really? You really expect me to go through that fucking hole?" I asked disbelievingly. *What do they do when heavyset people come through the haunted house? How do they fit?* I wondered.

This is creeping me the fuck out. Fucking Freya, I swear I'm going to kill her myself when all of this is said and done…

"It's the only way out," the girl said again. She was staring at the locked door.

"Do I need to unlock it for the next…customer?" I asked irritably.

"No, please don't," she whimpered.

Sighing, I squatted down in front of the trap door. A thin sheaf of plywood covered the tiny, square opening. I pushed on it with my palms, easily collapsing the board. I stared at the tight black hole before me. I had no choice but to crawl through.

Chapter Thirty-Three

Like a snake, I scurried through the tight tunnel in the dark, using my elbows and knees to guide me. *Ever been down the rabbit hole?* I imagined Freya asking, blowing smoke rings in the dark.

In less than a minute, I was in the next room. I stood up, brushing off my shorts and looking around. *God, all I want to do is find Freya,* I thought desperately. *Better yet, I want to get out of here and go see Rachel. Fuck Freya and all the trouble she's caused me.*

I considered shouting for Freya again, but didn't want to alert the creepy clown to my location. Even though none of this was real, I still felt mildly frightened.

There were more flashing lights in this room. They buzzed on and off, providing brief flashes of my surroundings.

There was no sound but the buzzing lights, but as I took a few steps forward in the dark, a loud speaker turned on, music blaring. I covered my hands with my ears, turning in circles, trying to find the source of the sound.

The music seemed to be coming from everywhere. I recognized the song immediately. An old seventies band, The Doors or something like that.

Lyrics rang out, words about riding snakes and kill kill kill…

I shuddered. *What was the point of all this?*

Wishing my eyes would adjust to the dark, I felt around for a wall. *Surely, if there was a trap door in the other room, there'll be one in here too. Right?*

Or better yet, maybe I just need to find the regular door and make a run for the stairs. Sure, the clown might chase me out of the haunted house, but it beat listening to this wild, crazy music in the pitch black darkness in this freaky place.

Still floundering through the flickering lights and booming music, I suddenly stopped dead in my tracks. I could "feel" someone in the room with me. I spun around in circles, waiting for the light to come on so I could see who or what was with me. But there was nothing but the pounding sounds of the guitar chords and Jim Morrison's haunting voice.

I inched along the wall, keeping my back pressed against it. *This isn't a normal haunted house.*

In fact, I was starting to wonder if I might be in some sort of real danger.

What sort of sick freaks design a haunted house in a place like this, anyway? *The same sort of weirdos who might actually hurt the girls who patronize it*, a voice in my head warned.

The light flicked on and off again, and I saw something crawling in the dark. I held my breath, edging toward the door, panicked. When the light flickered on again, I saw the clown's face. He was crawling on the floor, headed straight for me, his mouth hanging open in a gruesome grin.

Instantly, my fight or flight kicked in—I chose flight—and I ran for what I hoped was the direction of the bedroom door. Sounds of screaming filled my head.

Fuck. This house. This whole damn town.

I realized that I was the one screaming.

I threw the door open and ran out to the hallway, my feet nearly slipping out from under me.

"Please, let me out of here!" I shrieked, racing down the hallway toward the stairs. But then the door to the first room flew open, and the man with the pins in his face stepped out. *But he's a friend,* my brain tried to tell me.

Suddenly, thick arms grabbed me around the middle, body slamming me face first to the ground. My face and mouth hit the hardwood floor with a sickening thud.

Head spinning, I tried to claw and kick as the clown dragged me back down the hallway. I tried to look up at "Pinner," call for help, but he was gone.

The clown yanked me inside a room, tossing me on my back.

The song stopped momentarily, but then immediately started over. Jim Morrison sung about the end and how his only friend was the end…

I let out a bloodcurdling scream, still trying to

kick and punch on my back.

He was on top of me now, slamming the back of my head against the rigid wood floors.

He was going to kill me.

I felt a sharp prick in my right arm. He was drugging me! I kicked and fought, ignoring the tearing pain in my arm.

But then my arms turned to Jell-O and my breathing slowed. I laid my cheek against the cold, hard floor, sucking in small gasps as I stared at a picture on the wall. It was the picture I'd drawn back in Lamison, the one that looked like a scary house.

The picture got smaller and smaller, until it was a tiny dot.

And then my world faded to black.

Chapter Thirty-Four

Wendi

Sweat beading my face, I jerked up in bed, stopping short of screaming. It was my first nightmare in a while, but having one never surprised me. Thirty years had come and gone. Yet still…I dreamt of their faces, that horrible town…and the lyrics of that eerie song.

What had I been dreaming of, anyway? I struggled to remember as I stood up, stretched, and made my way to the kitchen. Marianna was sitting in a kitchen chair, her back facing me. Dressed in a silky, baby blue robe, she was working hard at something, sifting through pages of reports, her ice-blonde hair covering half her face as she wrote.

Five years had come and gone since our first meeting. She'd matured, aged even. Based on my own age, I was more of a mother to her, but she called me her friend.

Taking the seat across from her, she shot me a worried look.

"You were dreaming again…Was it about Flocksdale?" she asked. Her bright azure eyes beamed at me.

I shrugged, reaching out to steal her coffee. I took a sip. Made a face at her. She always used too much sugar.

Marianna had no one but me. And…the others, of course.

We'd formed a club of sorts. The "Lost Girls," we called ourselves.

Thanks to my late husband's position as a police sergeant, I still had connections in the police force. For the past several years, "the club" had been following all reported missing persons cases coming through the system, specifically missing teenage girls.

Ever since we burned down half of Flocksdale, the evil in that town had been lying low. Not one of the cases we'd followed up on could be linked to Flocksdale. Yet, we still met weekly to discuss the cases we'd each reviewed.

Truth be told, I'd have given it up years ago—if it weren't for Marianna. She was obsessed, pressuring me to bring as many copies of case files as I could manage.

"We need to talk," I said firmly, returning her mug of coffee. It was time to tell her—all of this needed to stop. She had plans to attend community college and I was working as an advocate for child sexual abuse victims. I loved my work and I wanted nothing more than for her to find something she loved to do just as much. This obsession with Flocksdale and missing girls was holding her back, stifling her.

I'd recently set her up with a counselor to work through some of the trauma and grief. I'd even tried taking her to the gun range, tried teaching her how to defend herself and let out some steam. But she'd missed her last few appointments, and nothing interested her besides Flocksdale and the possibility of linking one of these cases to the town that nearly destroyed both of us.

"Listen, Marianna—"

"No, wait. Me first," she interrupted, ruffling papers. She lifted up a missing persons report. It looked like any other. My reading glasses were in the bedroom, so I had to take it from her hands and squint at the tiny printed lines.

I skimmed it, sat the paper down. "Okay, what is it about this case? What makes you think it's linked to Flocksdale this time?" I didn't mean to sound condescending, but that's exactly how it came out.

Marianna narrowed her eyes at me, but explained, "This girl, Josie Crowley…she went missing a week ago from a town called Lamison Point. That's—"

"Far away from Flocksdale," I finished for her, sighing. I stood up, moving around the kitchen as she rambled on.

"Here's the thing, though. She took off after another incident…another girl—her friend, apparently—went missing several days before."

"They probably ran away together, like the last ten cases we looked into," I protested, pulling out an expired carton of eggs.

"Will you let me finish?" she shouted, slamming her fist down on the table. I stared at her, shocked by the outburst.

I set the spoiled eggs down and leaned against the counter, listening.

"The night before the first girl—Freya was her name—went missing, the girls were hanging out at a local carnival. The Carnival de Arcanorum—"

"The Carnival of Secrets," I said, crossing my arms over my chest. Marianna gave me a surprised look. "I studied a little Latin while in rehab," I said defensively.

"Instead of hanging out with her friend, Josie, Freya ditched her for a carnival worker. Josie was mad, so she left Freya there. Needless to say, Freya never turned up at school the next day. And when Josie went back to the carnival, the carnival had skipped town."

I gestured for her to continue.

"Josie was cooperating with the police. Telling them everything she knew…and then she turned up missing too. Only, in her case, she called her parents a couple days later. She told them that she had to find Freya and she was following a lead of sorts…"

"This still doesn't sound like anything the police can't handle, Marianna. I thought you were going to fill out those apps—"

"I'm not done," she reminded me again, giving me an icy cold glare. "Right before she took off, Josie went to her local librarian, asking for help finding an author. She wasn't sure it was relevant at the time, but that librarian recently came forward—after weeks of no sign or word from Josie—and she told the parents the name of the author Josie was so intent on finding."

Frustrated, I went back to the spoiled eggs. I took down an earthenware bowl. Started cracking away.

"According to the librarian, Josie said that if she could track down the author, she could find the carnival. So the author must have worked at the carnival, right? Well, the writer's name was Lucinda Livingston."

I suddenly remembered my dream. Less of a dream, and more of a memory…Marianna's face in that tiny window, like my own face reflecting back at me…I'd nearly burned the house down with her in it. I was trying so hard to destroy Flocksdale that I nearly destroyed her too. *Maybe I've already destroyed her by bringing her here with me, turning my obsession into hers.*

I was barely listening now. "Wendi, did you hear what I just said?"

"I'm sorry…what?" I asked, shattering the egg's delicate shell on the hard, unbreakable bowl.

"I tracked her down…the author she mentioned. Turns out, she really is an author. And guess where she's from? A tiny northeastern town, a town barely anyone's heard of. You might know it…" she said, shuffling through her papers.

I turned around, giving her my full attention.

"It's about time you listened," Marianna said, her icy blue eyes boring holes into mine. She was no longer ruffling papers, but staring at me intently.

She was holding a piece of paper in her hand, gripping it so tightly I could see the veins in her hand.

"Flocksdale," we said in unison.

My body jerked, bumping the edge of the bowl with my elbow. I watched the bowl crash to the ground, shattering into a million pieces, runny bits of egg leaking all over the kitchen floor.

Chapter Thirty-Five

"This is what we've been waiting for. I mean…I knew they'd strike again, but I didn't expect it to happen so soon, or that we'd be able to catch them," I said, more to myself than to Marianna.

We'd packed two suitcases full of clothes and toiletries. My brand new Corolla was filled with gas. Now all we had to do was drive to Flocksdale.

"Don't you think we should call the others? Ask them to come with us? Suzie Q or Matilda…"

I shook my head. "Listen, Marianna. This isn't a game anymore, or some sort of dinner theater show. These girls are in real danger and I don't want to bring anyone else along, taking a chance of endangering them too."

"Those girls—their names are Josie and Freya," Marianna said, staring out the window as we pulled away from our small two-bedroom apartment.

I knew she was pissed at me. She'd done all the legwork and now I was taking charge, bossing her around like a mother instead of her friend. As usual.

"I'm sorry I didn't take you seriously. I just didn't want you so fixated on Flocksdale. I want you to go to college and make something of yourself, Marianna. I don't want you to spend the rest of your life chasing demons like I did…"

"They're not just your demons, Wendi. They're mine too," she whispered, her voice cracking. I knew she was thinking about her family and my heart ached for her.

Reaching across the gear shift, I placed my hand on hers. "I know. I'm sorry, I know…"

After an hour of riding in silence, I pulled off at an abandoned rest area. "Can you pull out that map? Help me figure out how to get there?" I asked, pointing at the glove box.

She'd been sulking, her eyes glassy the whole ride so far.

She pulled the map out, unfolded it across her lap. Tracing the lines with her finger, she pondered for a minute. "We're at least a day's drive away," she remarked.

"Can you guide me from here?" I asked curiously. She nodded, pulling out her phone to access MapQuest.

I pulled back on the ramp, following the familiar highway signs as Marianna plotted out our trip and reviewed her copies of the case notes.

I knew the way to Flocksdale like the back of my hand. It was only last year, when Marianna and one of the other girls took a three day trip to Gatlinburg, that I drove this same route to Flocksdale. I stayed a few days, sleeping in my car, crouched in my seat with binoculars. I was just as obsessed as she was, only I did a better job of hiding it.

For now, I pretended not to know the way…giving her a task to keep her mind occupied. My mind, on the other hand, was full of hate. Hate for the sons of bitches responsible for hurting so many girls and their families. For hurting Marianna. For hurting me. The evil surrounding that town just wouldn't go away, no matter how hard I tried to force it to.

If they were at it again, trafficking drugs and girls, I was going to put a stop to it—again. Maybe this time I'd stop those fuckers for good.

Chapter Thirty-Six

Focusing on the map proved to be a good distraction for Marianna. We were getting close, only minutes away from the welcome sign to Flocksdale—a sign we thought we'd never see again when we left five years ago.

She'd perked up for the last few hours of the trip, showing me pictures of the missing girls and discussing the evidence objectively. But as we passed through a dark tunnel of trees, approaching the town of Flocksdale, her entire demeanor changed.

She was quiet, almost mute, her body stiffening in the seat across from me. The tension was so thick I could have sliced through it with a knife.

"It's okay. I brought plenty of guns and ammo, as usual," I tried to joke. But her lips were pursed, her brows knitted together in worry.

"Welcome to Flocksdale," she whispered as we pulled into the familiar town. Businesses were dark, the townspeople retired for the day. The town was so small, a population of less than three hundred residents. *Hard to believe so much evil could dwell here*, I thought drearily.

Within minutes, we'd passed the business district and were headed into rural territory. When I lived here as a kid, the houses were normal—ranch style dwellings and shotguns. But then the town rebuilt after half of the town was demolished, choosing an odd stilts design used to survive flooding in case the river ever got too high.

Flooding should be the least of this town's worries, I thought, shaking my head.

"What is it?" Marianna asked, a panicked quality to her voice as she watched my head shake from side to side.

"Just thinking, is all…about this stupid fucking town and all of the evil that dwells here. *Breeds* here, I should say."

She said nothing, staring straight ahead. We were both looking for it—the river. Five years ago, the town was on fire. The aftermath was obvious, some of the old houses on stilts stood tall, while others were blackened and decrepit, and still others looked freshly rebuilt.

"The evil around here is very old, sort of old, and modern. One generation after another…" Marianna said ominously. I understood what she meant completely. Generations of evil were here, and no matter how many times we tried to knock it down and burn it to the ground, the evil seemed to remain. As though evil people were drawn to this tiny rural town in the middle of nowhere.

We saw the river at the same time. Marianna drew in a sharp breath, then didn't seem to breathe anymore as we got closer. The houses were mostly dark. It felt as though they were watching us…like they always knew we'd come back for them.

I took a familiar turn on Lincoln Boulevard, heading for Clemmons Street—the street where the House of Horrors had always stood, no matter how many times we tried to destroy it.

What we saw came as a surprise. There were no houses on Clemmons Street or the street over—Brywood—either. But what we did see made my heart leap with fear and relief. A carnival—just like the one described in Lamison Point. Workers were taking down tents and sweeping the streets, disassembling rides.

"Looks like the freaks came home to roost," I murmured, my mouth dry.

Chapter Thirty-Seven

Josie

Someone stabbed me.

No, not stabbed…it didn't hurt enough to be a knife.

Poked. Someone poked me. *Another needle, perhaps?*

I jerked my eyes open, tried to move. My arms were restrained to a chair. So were my legs.

My thoughts raced. Too fast for me to follow their content.

I shifted around frantically, fighting to loosen the straps. I rocked back and forth, flexed against the tight leather binding. Clenched my jaw and growled.

Instead of breaking away from the chair, I knocked it over. It hit the ground with a loud thud, but not as loud as my right temple smacking against the wood floor beside it.

It didn't hurt. I felt no pain…

I had a sideways view of the room now. My eyes so wide they might rip and tear, splitting my caruncle.

Caruncle? I remembered once learning the anatomy of the eye. In Mrs. Delbert's biology class. Last semester. I sat next to Ricky Sanders. And Robin Tuchi. Behind me in my row were Allison Blackstone, Tommy Nuck, and Grant Johnson. And…

My eyes. Iris, pupil, sclera…caruncle, the tiny little red thing in the corner of my eye.

A light buzzed…On. Off. On and off again. I counted the buzzes, but couldn't see the light source. Why do lights make sound? And…how come I've never asked that question before?

What is wrong with me?

What the fuck sort of drug is this?

The door to the room opened. I watched a pair of size ten boots enter the room.

They stomped toward me, the sounds of each step vibrating my head—my head that didn't hurt one bit.

There's blood…I can taste it. Pouring down my face, streaming into my open mouth. *Why does blood taste like old pennies? And why doesn't anything hurt?*

The boots were in front of my face now, inches away from my nose. I caught a whiff of that dirty smell…the one people get when they never wear socks.

I didn't move. I wasn't afraid.

"Bring it on, motherfucker," I snarled.

Chapter Thirty-Eight

Suddenly, I was turned upright, my eyes instantly focused on Joseph's face. And others…

We were in the same bedroom, the one where the clown…

I shivered despite the warmth of my skin.

"Finally awake, are ya? I thought that brown would kill you, I did…Chuckles here almost overdosed ya, so I gave you something to wake you up a bit. Stupid, stupid," he scolded someone in the dark.

My mouth ached, but it didn't hurt. It felt sore, like I'd been punched. My entire face felt numb, now that I thought about it.

The clown was lying in the corner, in some weird sort of fetal position. Joseph was smacking the top of his bald, painted head. "Stupid, stupid…"

A strange sound escaped from the clown's mouth, like a child whimpering. I suddenly realized that he was mentally impaired. I tried to feel sorry for him, muster up some sympathy. Came up empty.

I moved my eyes around, looking for Pinner. He was sitting back on his haunches, having a smoke. Flicking ashes on the floor. Staring at me, as though he'd been waiting for me to see him.

"I told you those ears were infected…"

I suddenly remembered, a sharp blade…sounds of my own fleshing tearing…

"I cut the infected part off," he said, stubbing out his butt on the floor.

I screamed, remembering…him cutting, the clown playing with half an ear lobe in the dark. Shaking it back and forth in his mouth like a dog's chew toy…

I screamed louder, a deep guttural release of sheer terror.

Joseph came, told me to shut up.

I didn't.

Something heavy and cold slammed into the back of my head.

And that's when everything went black.

Chapter Thirty-Nine

"Wake up! Please wake up!" someone hissed in the dark. My eyes shot open, immediately sensing the drug in my system, but with lesser effects.

"Get. Up. Now."

I reached out in the dark—my arms no longer restrained—and grabbed a hold of somebody's arm. "Please, help…" I croaked, my throat hoarse.

"I'm trying. But we have to go. Now." Evan's face loomed close to mine.

But it was his dad…His friends from the carnival…

I had no other choice but to trust him.

I let him help me up in the dark. I stared at the crusty blanket I'd been laying on. It looked brown…dried blood smeared across where my head had been.

I was upstairs, still in the same room. I remembered my ears, the crying clown…something metal knocking me out in the dark…

My legs and feet felt wobbly. I gripped Evan's arm for support. "Everyone's asleep or gone home. But Pinner and Pockets are downstairs, so we have to sneak past them."

He opened the door to the room, peeked out. Motioned for me to follow him.

We lurked in the dark, taking small, tentative steps toward the staircase.

"Let me go first. If it's still all clear, I'll motion you down."

I stood at the top, painfully listening to each step he took—each movement creating a sharp, creaking sound.

I nervously stepped down the first few steps, peering around the twisted corner. My head was spinning. Evan stood at the bottom, surrounded by dim lights in the foyer. He motioned for me to come on down.

Biting my lip, I crept slowly, carefully. I finally understood that expression about stomachs and how they can be full of knots.

All I had to do was make it downstairs and the door to freedom was a few feet away.

I recited a familiar prayer, all the way to the bottom. Taking my hand, Evan walked me to the front door. I didn't bother looking around. My eyes were glued to my one chance of staying alive.

Carefully, he unlatched the bolt and quietly opened the door. Before he could say or do anything, I took off through the narrow gap, running down Clemmons Street.

Chapter Forty

I had superhuman strength. Unstoppable. I raced down the street, watching my feet move in blurring motions across the black top. Pounding the blacktop into oblivion.

Fuck this town. I won't stop running until I'm out of here forever. I don't care about Freya. About Evan. About anyone in this god forsaken place…I just want to go home, to my dad. To Candy. To my school and my old life.

To…Rachel.

I skidded to a stop. Where was Rachel? Had they taken her too? I whipped around in the dark, the ice cold October wind that felt more like December sliced through me, rippling shivers racing up my spine.

There were no houses in sight. But why would there be? No one was crazy enough to live close to the House of Horrors.

I could see Evan, running in the dark. Chasing me.

But why would he save me from there, just to

chase me again? That didn't make sense. I stepped forward, staring at him as he approached.

He stopped in front of me, gasping for breath, his face nearly as red as mine must have been.

"Please. Wait," he wheezed.

"Where is Rachel?" I asked, shoving him hard in the chest. He stumbled back, nearly falling.

"What? Rachel?" he asked, looking hurt by my push and confused by my question.

"Where is Rachel?" I repeated.

"She's at home," he said, looking around nervously. "She thinks you skipped town."

"And Freya?" I asked, preparing to shove him again to get answers.

At the mention of Freya's name, he froze.

He took a deep breath, staring at me strangely.

"I killed her," he said.

Chapter Forty-One

Fight or flight—this time fight won. I socked him in the face, my knuckles connecting with bone. I heard the sound of his nose cracking, so I punched him again and again, trying to crack his entire face.

"Please, please…" he whined, bent down protecting his head and face now.

We were standing in the middle of the street, no signs or sounds of people. As much as I wanted to kill him, I didn't have a weapon and I needed to go. Now.

I had to get somewhere, find help…*I need to go to Rachel's*, I decided.

"Wait. Don't run. Let me explain," Evan whimpered, clutching his nose. Blood seeped through the gaps in his fingers, dripping down the backs of his hands and forearms.

"I had no other choice. I had to get you here. I had her tied up. But she ran. She ran and ran. And somebody had to stop her, control her…"

"What do you mean, get *me* here?" I shouted. The sound of my voice echoed down the deserted street, reminding me that I needed to go.

I didn't have time for explanations. Nor did I care. If Freya was dead, I needed to get out of here. Out of Flocksdale before I ended up dead too.

I turned on my heels and took off running. I never should have stopped in the first place.

"You're my sister!" Evan croaked from behind me.

I guess this is the part where I should have stopped. Where I should have asked, "What? Why? How?"

But I kept on going, trying to wrap my brain around his words as I did.

Chapter Forty-Two

I heard shouts coming from behind me, voices not belonging to Evan. I veered off Lincoln Boulevard, and bolted through somebody's yard. Motion lights flashed on, illuminating my path and alerting my enemies.

I didn't look back.

A gunshot rang out in the distance, startling me enough to stop. I ducked behind a child's playhouse, looking around crazily.

My thoughts were still racing from the meth, I presumed. I sucked in breaths.

Who has a gun? Surely not Evan, or he would have stopped me earlier.

I listened in the dark, holding my breath.

Distant shouts were becoming less distant.

I looked around, gathering my thoughts. I needed to head toward the business district. Away from this demented town.

Out was west. I imagined Jim Morrison's voice,

singing that devastating song in that dark room. A lyric about the west being the best.

"Yes, it is," I muttered, taking off in that direction.

I made it three more blocks. I was getting closer to town. I pressed my back against the side of an abandoned skating rink, peering around the corner.

Again, I listened. Were they coming this way?

A twig snapped behind me. I whirled around just in time to see Pockets' ugly, disfigured face.

He grabbed me in a bear hug, carrying me—kicking and screaming—toward what looked like a limousine in the dark.

Chapter Forty-Three

Marianna

I was tired. Hungry. But that wasn't important right now. All that mattered was finding Freya and Josie. Wendi had insisted we go back and stay in a hotel tonight, despite my unending arguments to the contrary. I wanted to go find them. Right now.

"You know as well as I do, we need to come up with a game plan," Wendi said, parking at a lousy Motel 6 in Mooresville. We weren't even staying in Flocksdale. *What good could we do from here? As far as we knew, Josie or Freya could be in trouble right now! Or worse yet, they could be dead already...*

"Come up with a game plan? You mean like you did all those years ago? Wait eight fucking years before you did something to the bastards that took you?" I shouted. As soon as the words were out, I regretted them.

Wendi had taken me in, been like a big sister/mother/friend all rolled into one, and now here I was…treating her like shit.

Wendi stared at me, unfazed by my cruel words.

"Marianna, I know…I know you want to run in there, guns blazing…and if that's what we have to do, then that's what we'll do. But it'll have to be tomorrow. We need to discuss our plans, find out everything we can before we just show up asking about those girls. If they took them or hurt them, they're not just going to admit it. We need to know where to start. Who to talk to first. Where to look…"

"Okay," I agreed. "And I'm sorry," I said, looking at my friend.

"It's okay," she said, smiling. "I know what it's like to be angry. I know how it feels to let anger take over, to fuel your entire body, to consume…just don't let it eat you whole, Marianna." She stared at me with an odd expression, full of sadness and pleading.

"I'll get the bags," I offered.

She checked us in while I unloaded our stuff. The hotel was deserted, two lone vehicles parked near the entrance. When she returned with the key, I followed her inside. We were on the top floor, room 301.

Inside, there were two twin-sized beds, a rickety desk, and a small, old-fashioned tube TV. I set our bags down, immediately heading for the desk. I pulled out my laptop, ready to search everything I could about the *Carnival de Arcanorum*, as it was supposedly called when it visited Lamison Point.

Wendi used the bathroom and came back out, taking a seat on the bed. She stared at me, watching me type in the search engine.

"What?" I raised my eyebrows at her. "Why are you looking at me like that?" I demanded, irritably.

She just smiled. "When Shelby left for college and Jonathan died, I felt this huge hole in my heart. Sure, she was still my daughter and I'd see her a few times a year while she was on break, but it still hurt like hell. I spent so much of my life focused on my hatred for Flocksdale, but then…when I had a family, everything shifted to them."

I closed the laptop, stared at her. She'd been through so much in her life and I never knew how to comfort her.

"But then you came along, and I found someone…like a daughter and friend all in one…and having you to take care of made me a better person. You're my best friend, Marianna. My best friend in the whole world."

Unable to hold back tears, I ran to her side. We sat on the bed, hugging. Crying.

"Okay. No more tears," Wendi finally said, leaning back and looking at me. She swiped a tear from my cheek. "I'm going to go get us something to eat. While I'm gone, I want you to find out every single thing you can. And when I get back, we'll come up with a plan."

"We could just order pizza," I suggested.

"Nah. I'm craving a hamburger, aren't you? All those years of working at McDonald's got me hooked," she said, grinning.

I nodded. A big greasy hamburger did sound

good. "Okay. Get my usual." I typed words in the search engine, barely looking up as she closed the hotel door behind her.

Chapter Forty-Four

After an hour of searching and finding very little about the carnival that originated from Flocksdale, I stood up to stretch. Glancing at the clock, I suddenly realized how long it had been since Wendi left. *What the hell was taking so long?*

I dug my cell phone out of my purse and speed dialed her number. I sat back down in front of the computer, waiting for it to ring.

I could hear another phone ringing in the bathroom. *Oh, shit! She left her phone!*

Groaning, I sauntered into the hotel bathroom, squinting around the room for the phone. There was another door inside, leading to a small attached toilet area.

The phone was sitting on a stack of clean, white towels. I picked it up, staring at my own missed call on the screen. Swiping the missed alert away, I saw the notes section open. It looked like a letter Wendi was working on…

I gasped, the words blurring on the phone. I had to grab the handicap bar to steady myself.

Dear Marianna,
If you love me as your mother and friend, please do this one thing for me. Call a cab and go home. I'll meet you there in a few days. And if by some chance I don't make it back…just please know that I love you, and tell my Shelby I love her. Go to college. Make babies. Live a life. A real life, not one centered on anger and vengeance and obsession. This is the end of Flocksdale. You'll never have to worry about that place again, I promise. It's almost over.
Don't become me.
Love you always and forever,
Wendi Wise

My hand shook, tears welling up in my eyes. Wendi had gone back to Flocksdale without me. She'd been planning it all along.

Chapter Forty-Five

Josie

When I came to, I was in a house…but not the House of Horrors I'd expected. Rather, I was in a rundown, wood-paneled living room in what appeared to be a shotgun house. I was sitting in another chair, but this time I wasn't strapped in. Grateful for small miracles, I suppose…

My hands were shaking as I reached up to touch my tender earlobes. Or what was left of them. Uneven strips of flesh were connected to my head, holes for ears but barely any skin or cartilage left attached…

I tried not to scream, sucking in deep breaths as I viewed my new surroundings. I was alone in the room.

I started to stand up, but someone wrapped an arm around my neck from behind.

"Sit still, princess," growled Pockets in my ear.

"Malachi and Joseph are on their way in. They had to deal with another…*problem.*"

My heart leapt at the word "problem," and it was almost like I knew.

A door behind me opened and I whipped around, watching in horror as the clown carried Rachel's lifeless body over one shoulder. Joseph and Malachi were behind him.

This time I couldn't hold it in anymore. I released an ear-piercing scream.

Chapter Forty-Six

Pockets silenced me, placing his thick, foul-smelling hands over my mouth and nose. Panicked, I kicked my legs and pulled at his hands, trying to free myself and catch a breath. I watched, my eyes widening in horror, as the crazy clown dropped Rachel's body in the corner next to a large piece of furniture covered in a tarp.

Her eyes were closed and her body limp, but suddenly, she let out a soft moan. Pockets released my mouth and I let out a sigh of relief. At least she was still alive!

But for how long, though? a voice in my head resounded.

"Why are you doing this?" I whined, staring straight at Joseph. He gripped the gun on his hip, flexing his jaw as he watched me.

"Look, we're trying to run a legitimate business here. I don't know why you're here, nosing around in my backroom, asking questions about some girl we've never heard of…"

"Your son admitted to killing her," I hissed. Malachi stood in the shadows, watching us interact, his arms calmly clasped behind his back.

Joseph looked back at Malachi, and then to Pockets.

"So, the idiot told ya, did he? Well, I don't know who's more stupid, him or you. We were going to rough you up a bit more, send ya packing, but now that you've said that…well, you've left me no other choice."

Joseph unholstered the gun, stuck its barrel in my face. The gun felt like hot ice, burning the tip of my nose with its cold, steel body.

Speaking of the "idiot," Evan came racing in. "Dad, Dad…you can't do this. You can't kill her…please," he begged.

Joseph stared at his son, rolling his eyes in disgust. He didn't lower the gun. "You brought this upon her, son. You brought this upon all of us. We're trying to get out of the sex trade, focus on the real money maker—drugs. I'll never understand why you took that girl, why you jeopardized everything for some stupid little slut."

I heard the click of the safety. My eyes shifted crazily, searching for a way out. Some sort of move to get me out of here.

"Because," Evan said, "I didn't do this for that girl—Freya, whatever her name was—I did this for her." He pointed a shaky finger at me, and we locked eyes. His eyes—they looked so much like my own. And his hair like my natural color…with the muddy, brown shade…but how? *How could he be my brother?*

My eyes fixated on Joseph. I said, "I'm your daughter. He wanted to bring me to you."

Chapter Forty-Seven

Of all the things Joseph expected to hear, news that I was his daughter certainly wasn't one of them. He dropped the gun to his side, mouth fallen open, staring at me with a twisted look of confusion and then understanding.

"I don't understand it, either," I said, looking back and forth between son and father.

"The journals…I read mom's journals. I've known for years, but I never expected to track her down. I found her profile on Facebook. It was that simple. And then I—"

"Insisted we visit a little, shitty town called Lamison Point," Malachi growled, stepping out from the shadows. He walked toward Evan, clutching the boy's shirt.

"What the fuck? You mean, she's my—cousin?" Pockets asked disbelievingly. He shook his head back and forth, disgusted. He didn't believe it. Didn't want to…

"How?" I squeaked. They all looked at me, nearly forgetting my presence in the room.

"My dad was in love with a woman named Brenda Crowley, a woman he sold drugs to and ran around with. Cheated on Mom with," Evan declared, staring at his dad hatefully. "She always knew. Always…but she didn't know Brenda got pregnant. She didn't know about your *daughter*," he said, looking at me with a mixture of hate and sadness.

Pockets was looking from Joseph to Evan, his face contorted in pain. Confusion.

Malachi was staring at me. "So, you're not the youngest living descendent of the Garretts then, are ya, Evan?" he asked bitterly, not taking his eyes off mine.

I stared back, wondering what this meant.

Joseph looked at me, raised the gun. He pointed it toward Evan's temple and pulled the trigger.

Chapter Forty-Eight

Skull fragments and tissue exploded through the air, covering my face and hands. Bits of a tooth embedded in my hand…

I let out a bloodcurdling scream then jumped up, running for the door.

Chapter Forty-Nine

The clown was on the case. He grabbed me around my waist, knocking me face first to the ground. My face and chest slammed against the thinly carpeted floor, and then he dragged me across the room, my cheeks on fire from the rug burn.

I dug my elbows and knees in, trying to slow down the inevitable. But he kept dragging, all the way to Rachel's crumpled figure on the floor.

Lying next to her now, I reached out to touch her face. Her face was battered, with bulging bruises on each eye and cheek. "Oh, Rachel…I'm so sorry…"

She was breathing. I could hear wheezing sounds from her chest. There was still a chance. The clown stood over me, gasping for air as he bent at the waist. His macabre white makeup was dripping from his face, melting away to show a normal-looking man. I kicked out with my left foot, caught him right in the groin. I took off crawling, trying to get up…but then Joseph's elbow came down over my head, knocking me back down, face first on the putrid-smelling carpet.

"Do you want to see our newest exhibit?" Malachi asked. He was standing over Evan's body—what used to be his body. His father didn't even flinch at his dead son's corpse.

Removing the tarp from what appeared to be a tall cabinet, I didn't know what I was looking at. It was one of those stupid displays, the ones I'd seen in the freak show tent, inside the creepy room of dead things.

It was half a girl, half a fish. Sort of like…a mermaid. I stared at the bloated eyes and nose, the coral-colored hair floating around her face. Tiny, dead arms curled up in front of her, a begging posture. She was topless, small breasts poking out beneath the array of wild hair. Around her waist was where they'd sewn the large fin on. The handiwork was pathetic.

The eyes, the hair…I stared at the mermaid's pouty red lips. "Nooooooo!" I screamed.

It was Freya.

Chapter Fifty

Wendi

I promised never to lie again, but I suppose that was a lie itself. I had to lie to Marianna. I couldn't risk losing her, not again. I saw myself within her—a damaged lost soul, cynical as hell and hell-bent on destroying everyone associated with Flocksdale. Everyone who tried to hurt me.

But I didn't want her to be like me—so I played the role of a liar. A role I'd played often, and well.

I'd downloaded the author's book—the one Josie mentioned to the librarian. The "Bearded Lady" as she was called in the freak show, had included pictures of herself on display at the show. In the background of one photo, I'd see a man. I didn't know the man, but in a sense, I did.

He was the spitting image of a man named Jed—a man who went to prison years ago. He was the man who kidnapped me in the limousine.

With technology these days, it only took me a few minutes to figure out his name and address.

Joseph Garrett lived in his father's old house. And the limousine was still registered in his father's name: Malachi Jed Garrett. All these years, I'd assumed he'd died in prison, but little did I know, he'd been released a couple years ago due to terminal cancer. His son, Joseph, and Joseph's children—if he had any—were the last living descendants of the Garretts. And surprise surprise—they were kidnapping young girls again.

There was a motel in Flocksdale we could have stayed at, but I had to get Marianna as far away from Flocksdale as I could manage without tipping her off. I only hoped that she'd be so busy researching, that it would be hours before she figured out what I was up to.

Before I went there, I drove to the House of Horrors. It sat silently, almost beautiful with the river glistening as its backdrop. Remnants of a carnival littered the streets surrounding it. But it sat alone, magnificent and awful in its own right. Half the house was scorched, as was the grass around it. Remnants of another botched attempt at destroying it.

I'd failed then, but I wouldn't fail now. Evil wasn't here tonight. The generation of evil had moved on. I drove toward Weston Street, looking for the house with the limo.

Tonight, the evil was going to end. Once and for all. I'd do whatever it took to put a stop to it, to save future generations of women and their families from the cruel torture inflicted by the Garretts and Flocksdale.

I parked my car against the curb, grazing

bumpers with the limousine. The last time I saw it, I was barely thirteen years old.

I got out. I was ready.

Approaching the ugly, dented limo, I ran my hands along its fenders and side panels. This damn car had appeared in so many of my nightmares, and here it sat—lame as could be.

I will no longer fear the Garretts. I tried to teach them not once, but twice already that they should fear *me*. Well, this time I wouldn't leave any survivors. No one would be left to fear me when I was done with these assholes.

Chapter Fifty-One

Marianna

I stood in the parking lot of the hotel, staring at the empty parking space where Wendi's Corolla had been. She'd taken the car, the guns, everything…

Thinking fast, I ran toward the two other vehicles in the lot. A small two-door Scion was locked tight. But the old pickup wasn't.

I wrenched open the door, jumping inside. There weren't any keys in the ignition. I slammed my palms against the wheel, frustrated.

I looked everywhere—under the floor mats, on top of the visor, in the ashtray, and under the seats.

Fuck.

I shoved the heavy truck door open, nearly tumbling out it was up so high. I slammed the door shut, paced the parking lot. Now what?

I came back to the truck, leaned against it. *I'll*

just call a cab, I considered. But that would take forever…

Or walk. But again, that would take too long. I stared at the stupid, redneck truck. Punched the fender and the fuel door.

But looking at the truck, I had a strange thought. A memory flashed—my real father, his hands rough with calluses, taking me into the grocery, sticking his keys inside the fuel door.

I reached out and opened the small circular portal. A key ring full of keys fell out on the ground.

"Thank you, Daddy," I whispered, sliding in behind the wheel.

Chapter Fifty-Two

I ripped and roared through the streets of Flocksdale, looking for Wendi's Corolla or anything to alert me to her whereabouts. The truck was a stick shift, and I had no idea what I was doing. The truck heaved and hoed, jerking forward crazily, and then dying at least ten times.

The lights to the House of Horrors weren't lit, and surprisingly there were no other houses on Clemmons Street anymore. I shuddered at the sight of my old home. The place that nearly killed me.

The *people* who nearly killed me, I corrected myself.

Deciding to drive toward Saints Road, I made a left…just as I heard the sound of gunshots being fired.

"Wendi!" I screamed, pressing my foot down hard on the gas. The truck stalled. Sputtered and died.

I jumped out, took off running. Following the

sounds of gunfire.
Following the sounds of Wendi Wise.

Chapter Fifty-Three

Josie

Rachel was waking up now. I lay on the floor beside her, stroking her hair and cheeks. I wept, rocking back and forth. I was waiting for them to kill us.

I tried not to look at the modern-day Fiji mermaid behind the glass. I tried to pretend it wasn't Freya.

"Where are we?" Rachel whimpered.

"Shhh. Just rest. Don't worry," I stupidly tried to console her.

"I think with a little more slicing and dicing by Pinner, we can turn you into our very own Elephant Girl! Just think, you won't have to be in a case. You'll get a prime-time spot in the very front row of the freak show," Malachi said, cackling evilly.

My stomach lurched. I fought the urge to throw up. "And you," he said, pointing at Rachel, "I still haven't decided what to do with you. We might just have a little fun with you first, then dump you in the river so your mother doesn't suspect."

Rachel tried to sit up, her lips parting slowly as she realized where she was and what was happening. I squeezed her hand, trying to calm her. She looked at me, her eyes filled with utter terror.

My mouth was dry. My limbs were numb. And Pinner was sharpening his knives.

Chapter Fifty-Four

A loud blast jarred my entire body. Shocked, I looked around frantically, still holding onto Rachel. The room instantly filled with smoke. "Come on!" I shouted, yanking her arm so hard I'm surprised I didn't rip it out of socket.

I dragged her behind me, stumbling through the smoke. "Don't fucking move," Pockets said, wrapping his arm around my throat.

"Go!" I shouted, shoving Rachel forward. She disappeared in the smoke, stumbling ahead. I coughed uncontrollably, trying to jerk out of Pockets' grasp. A loud bang, another gunshot…a hole in Pockets' head.

His grip on me loosened, and he tumbled to the floor like a sack of potatoes. I placed a hand over my face and mouth, eyes burning. Someone with a gas mask was pulling me by the elbow.

"Follow me," said the person in the mask, the sounds of the words garbled, distorted.

I didn't care who this person was, they had to be safer than the Garretts. I stumbled through the house, trying to keep up with the mask-wearer.

More shots rang out. I looked up, squinted. The man in the mask had a gun in each hand. He shot the clown between the eyes.

My eyes were on the door. I could see it through a hazy cloud of smoke up ahead. I had to get to Rachel.

Finally through the front door, I sucked in desperate breaths of air, screeching her name in the dark.

Then suddenly, someone grabbed me from behind. Started dragging me back toward that wretched limo. My eyes caught sight of Rachel, running away in the distance.

Yes, run! Run away! I thought happily, giddily.

"Stop! Stop right there!" someone shouted. It was a girl, no older than twenty, racing across the lawn toward me. I jerked around, trying to see who my captor was. It was Pinner. *They should rename him the Butcher*, I thought, shaking fearfully. I twisted and pulled, tried to kick him in the shins from behind.

He was gripping me so tightly, I could feel dozens of piercings on his chest digging into my backside.

"Let her go!" the blonde girl shouted, stopping less than a few feet from us. She didn't have a weapon that I could see.

Pinner laughed. Clutching me with one hand, he opened the door to the limo, preparing to toss me inside, like they did last time.

"Not this fucking time," someone said. The person in the mask ran out of the foggy house, gun aimed straight at his head.

With no hesitation, the mask-wearer pulled the trigger. Bullets rang out as he shot him again and again. Pinner fell against that awful limo, his dead body jerking from side to side as the mask-wearer shot him. *How do you like that metal in your chest?* I thought, unflinching as I watched him die.

When he was finished, the mask-wearer dropped the gun, yanking the gas mask off.

But it wasn't a *he*.

"Wendi!" the blonde girl shouted, running toward her friend. They embraced.

"Are you okay?" the woman named Wendi asked, walking toward me. I was still in shock, my body reeling.

"We need to go now," she said hurriedly, not waiting for me to respond. "Everybody in the car!" She pushed us toward her Corolla.

Painfully, I climbed in behind the young blonde. Wendi leaned inside. "I have to go back in. Joseph's still in there. I'm sorry," she said, slamming the door to the car.

She raced back inside the smoke-filled house.

"No!" the other girl shouted, fighting to get out of the door. Child locks were on. She climbed through the front, kicking me in the process. I wasn't sure what to do, but I couldn't let them go it alone. It hurt like hell, but I climbed over the seat behind her, dragging myself out of the car. I ran behind the blonde girl, trying to shout for her to wait.

But before I could even reach the front door, Wendi was stumbling back out. The other girl screamed and then caught her in her arms. She was bleeding profusely, a gaping wound in her chest.

There was a gun on the ground beside her. I picked it up and ran inside, determined to shoot that bastard myself. But two steps in, I found him. Joseph was already dead. They must have shot each other in the process.

Police sirens roared in the distance, blessedly close but not close enough.

Chapter Fifty-Five

Wendi

Malachi was dead. Joseph was dead. The bizarre clown. The other man, the one with the disfigured face, was dead too. They were *all* dead. The last of the Garrett family...

When I ran back outside the smoke-filled house, the first faces I saw were Marianna's and Josie's. I was so happy to see them safe. Their expressions changed from thrilled to devastated.

Marianna was staring at my chest. I followed her piercing blue eyes, stared at the gaping red hole in my own chest.

My body slammed against the ground, shaking. I couldn't feel pain, but my head felt foggy and strange. I stared at the sky, a bed of moon-lined clouds...like a beautiful painting in a museum or a lovely screen saver I used to have...

This is not a scene...this is my life, I realized.

And I could feel the life draining out of me.

I'm dying.

I moved my eyes side to side, catching a glimpse of Marianna. She leaned over me, her eyes wide and full of pain.

I tried to move my mouth and form the words—words she'd heard a million times, but I needed to say them. But she said them for me…

"I love you, Wendi. Please don't die," she whispered, rocking my body back and forth, although I couldn't feel her touch.

I coughed and sputtered. Too much blood was coming out, choking me and stealing my breath.

Yanking off her shirt, Marianna tried to plug my wound. She always tried so hard to fix me, all the while I was trying to fix her too.

Perhaps we were put on this Earth to fix each other…

My body convulsed.

For most of my life, when I closed my eyes, all I could hear was that dreadful song—that song, the one they played in the House of Horrors. But for the first time since I was a young child, there was nothing but silence and the cool, sweet breath of the night air hugging my body. Everything bad and painful falling away…

I closed my eyes. I could feel my grandmother's hands—paper thin, but rough on the tips from her sewing—she was rubbing my wounds away. And the sounds of my father's old steel guitar and my mother's singsong voice, telling me all would be okay. And my daughter, Shelby…I could see her in my arms, a newborn baby, her eyes latching onto mine as we fell in love for the first time.

Moments. So many beautiful moments in my life.

And then I thought about Jonathan and saw his perfect face, the way he always looked at me in a way I knew I was loved…and I smiled.

My eyes fluttered open one last time. To say goodbye to the girl who had become not only my best friend but my daughter, sister, and friend all rolled into one. She was a better version of me. Better than I could have ever hoped to be.

"Marianna…don't become what they want you to be. Don't become me. Don't become me."

Chapter Fifty-Six

Marianna

Wendi was wrong. I did become her. I became all the parts of her she couldn't see…all the parts that I loved. Her goodness, loyalty, and love. Her perseverance and strength.

I didn't want her to die in Flocksdale. But apparently, it's what she wanted all along. As much pain and horror as she experienced there, she also met the love of her life and gave birth to her daughter there.

She was buried on a rainy Monday morning in Flocksdale's cemetery, next to her husband and hero, Jonathan. She wanted to put an end to the violence and evil, and she did…but she gave up her life doing so. And Wendi wouldn't have wanted it any other way. No one else was up to the job, and so she stood up and accomplished it herself. Just as she always did.

I'm going to college next year, a couple states over from where Josie's going to art school. I have no one now that Wendi's gone and my business in Flocksdale is done. Although I'm sad, this is exactly what Wendi wanted. Now I have no choice but to follow through with her plans. Make a life for myself. Find someone and make babies. And that's exactly what I plan to do.

Chapter Fifty-Seven

Josie

I am the last living descendent of the Garrett family, the only proof that that horrendous family ever existed, through some glitch in the evolution chain. I didn't want to tell my father the truth about my mother's indiscretions, but I had to. And surprisingly, he already knew.

Although I should hate my mother for what she did—cheating on my dad and going to jail—I don't. She left me in the hands of my wonderful father, and for that, I'll be forever grateful. I'm learning to appreciate Candy, although sometimes it's an uphill battle.

Rachel and Lucy come to visit often. I'm going to art school next year, and after that, who knows? The world awaits, I suppose.

As the last Garrett, I thought my family name would become my downfall. But instead, it became my windfall. All of that evil money—from the drugs and the girls—fell into my lap one cold winter day, as a lawyer sat in my living room, telling me and my dad I was rich. Rich beyond our wildest dreams.

I have no idea what I'll do with the money. The leftover money, that is. I spent over ten million of it purchasing my own town. A little town you might have heard of…

Nobody lives there now, but it's full of places where people can shop and eat. Wendi and her husband are buried there. Their daughter doesn't live too far away, so she visits them often. Marianna and I also organized several women's shelters and help centers, and spread them throughout the district.

I never knew Wendi in life. But in death, I'd like to think she's proud.

Epilogue

In late 2015, the town of Flocksdale finally met its maker. The remaining residents were bought out, the houses torn to the ground—for the last and final time. The businesses were demolished, replaced with a strip mall, movie theater, and fun park. Restaurants and night clubs line the river. Shelters and centers offering services to women sparkle like neon beacons of light.

"Come find me," I imagine Wendi whispering through the trees. "Come find me and I will help…"

In a sense, with all the bright new attractions, it was almost easy to forget…

To forget that evil once dwelled there, like a living, breathing, *breeding* thing…

But that's the thing about evil. Evil is not a thing.

It's not a house or a building…or even a town.

Evil is all around us. Inside some people. And sometimes, inside ourselves…

But we won't let it in…not us. We are strong. We are resilient. We are the lost girls, and we're always watching you…

Acknowledgements

To all of my readers—thank you for supporting me and making my dreams come true. Just knowing I have people who want to read my books makes me so happy and makes my days just that much brighter.

To my amazing street team, Flocksdale's Finest—thank you guys so much for being such amazing fans and friends. I wouldn't give you guys up for the world.

To all of my friends named Rachel—I'm so lucky to have so many Rachels in my life and I appreciate each and every one of you guys.

To my husband—thank you for putting up with all of my writing and being my biggest fan every step of the way.

To my children—thank you for making my life meaningful and for inspiring me every day to be someone who makes you proud.

To Limitless Publishing—thank you for allowing me to tell this story, and for believing in me as a writer.

To Toni—thank you for fixing my small (and huge) mistakes. I don't know what I'd do without you.

To Lydia and Crystal—thank you for working hard every day to promote my books.

To Ashley Byland—thank you for your amazing concepts and designs with the cover art. You bring my characters to life and I can't thank you enough for that.

To all of the Limitless staff I've left out—you

guys rock! Go Team Limitless! I appreciate each and every one of you.

To my mother, father, and sister—I love you guys so much! Thanks for being my family.

About the Author

Besides my family, my greatest love in life is books. Reading them, writing them, holding them, smelling them…well, you get the idea. I've always loved to read, and some of my earliest childhood memories are me, tucked away in my room, lost in a good book. I received a five dollar allowance each week, and I always—always—spent it on books. My love affair with writing started early, but it mostly involved journaling and writing silly poems. Several years ago, I didn't have a book to read so I decided on a whim to write my own story, something I'd like to read. It turned out to be harder than I thought, but from that point on I was hooked. My first and second books were released by Sarah Book Publishing: This Is Not About Love and Grayson's Ridge. I'm a total genre-hopper. Basically, I like to write what I like to read: a little bit of everything! I reside in Floyds Knobs, Indiana with my husband, three children, and massive collection of books. I have a degree in psychology and worked as a counselor.

Facebook:
https://www.facebook.com/CarissaAnnLynchauthor

Twitter:
https://twitter.com/carissaannlynch

Goodreads:
https://www.goodreads.com/author/show/11204582
.Carissa_Lynch

Blog:
https://carissaannlynch.wordpress.com/